Love in the Air

Gail Gaymer Martin

ISBN-13: 978-1-947523-02-9
ISBN-10: 1-947523-02-3

Chapter 1

"Amazing beauty, but what I really need is adventure." A raw sigh sailed from her lungs.

Allysa Grant stood in front of Bell Rock, gazing at the morning sunrise. The sight never failed to thrill her as it rose above the red rocks of Sedona turning the rocks into gold. She drew in a breath, so glad she'd moved from Indiana with the encouragement of her good friend Marcy who finally persuaded her to apply for a position at the Verde Valley Medical center in Cottonwood where Marcy lived. Yet always seeking adventure, Ally's vision of life in the Southwest aroused her interest. The more she pictured it, the more she wanted to live in Sedona and add a red rock escapade to her life.

With another new idea skipping through her mind, she powered her way along the trail, for a hike around Bell Rock and Courthouse Butte, but something motivated her to slow her steps. She paused and looked up again. As her heart skipped, her focus remained glued to the sky.

"Thank you." Embarrassed, she turned to see if anyone was nearby and heard her speak out loud. She'd meant it as a prayer. Her gaze shifted from the lovely sight of the rising sun to another glorious spectacle.

Two hot air balloons swept along in the breeze, the large wicker baskets holding eager people waving from above as they experienced a very special way to enjoy the red rocks, the clusters of trees and cacti that dotted the rolling hillsides.

As she studied the sight, her drive for a new experience rose. One day soon, a balloon would sweep into the air with her riding in the basket. Adventure was her middle name. At least, that's what she'd always said.

She started the trek around Bell Rock, but the hike was ruined by her preoccupation with staring at the brightly colored balloons hanging aloft in the blue and golden-specked sky. Instead of continuing the journey around Courthouse Butte, she took the Rector Trail back to her starting point and headed home.

As she jaunted back toward her condo, she nodded a greeting to those who passed. Friendliness she'd learned, was a trait of the Villagers. No matter where she went, someone would stop to say hello or ask what state she was from. Though an unusual phenomena compared to her home in the Midwest, many people now living in the area had once visited Sedona, and as she had done had then decided to make it their permanent home.

Marcy begged her to find an apartment or condo in Cottonwood since it was where they both worked, but the drive was little more than twenty-five minutes to the town, so why miss the beauty that surrounded her in the Village of Oak Creek, the southern end of Sedona?

With a rare day off, she slowed her pace and enjoyed the morning's cooler temperatures. A breeze brushed her cheeks and touched her arms as it often did in the morning. Soon the heat of summer would be upon them when breezes were as rare as days off.

As she jogged up Jack's Canyon Road and approached Cortez Drive, she pulled out her cell phone and hit Marcy's number. After five rings, she gave up and left voice mail. "Call me when you can. I'd like to invite you to join me on an adventure." She chuckled at the useless comment. Marcy disliked her eagerness for exploration of new experiences, yet she'd often coerced Marcy to join her, and on occasion Marcy actually enjoyed herself.

A breeze whispered along her skin again, and though near her condo, she nudged herself to keep going. She loved walking up the incline on Jack's Canyon Road, especially on such a perfect day as it was. The roadway ascended toward Lee Mountain, and she pushed herself to keep trudging upward. The walk back was downhill, and she would enjoy the easier trek back. She passed Canyon Mesa community, and soon she passed a multitude of residences as the scene thinned to an open landscape. She glanced above to see if the balloons were still in sight. Either they'd landed or were hidden behind the rocky landscape.

Amid the acres of grass and desert, she spotted a horse and rider near a ranch house with a barn and stable in the open land. She paused to watch, but when he rode her way, she spun around and headed further up the highway. Though she tried to pick up her pace, horse's hooves sounded behind her, and she reprimanded herself for acting so foolish. She had every right to be on the road…and to stop even to see the view including a horse and rider. Yet, the sound of hooves addled her anyway.

Within seconds, the horse and rider trotted alongside her and stayed there. Finally, she glanced up into the rider's gorgeous sky-blue eyes. Her tongue stuck to the roof of her mouth, blaming her dry mouth on forgetting to bring a bottle of water. She shifted her gaze to the horse as she worked to get her mouth unglued. "Good Morning." She managed a faint smile. "You have a beautiful horse."

His eyes searched hers. "Thanks. It's a quarter horse." He gave the horse's thick mane a pat. "Horses need exercise, so I try to ride them by taking a different one out each day. Sometimes I ride them more than once a day…at least when I can."

"How many horses do you own?" She shifted her eyes toward the ranch. Besides the house and a barn, she turned her attention to a large stable. "You must own many horses."

"I have four right now. But I board horses, too, so I have a few more in the stable. Obviously those are not mine." He waved his hand toward the stable.

She tried to comply to the motion, but she'd already viewed the stable. Instead, she studied his handsome face. His tanned skin blended with his wavy medium brown hair with red highlights almost the same shade as the horse. "What color is this horse?"

"It's sorrel which is obviously a brownish red." He dropped his gaze to the horse and then back to her. "Do you like the color?"

"I do. It's very pretty, sort of calming, like the sun reflecting on rich soil."

"Rather poetic." He grinned. "Are you a writer?"

She drew back and poked her chest. "Me? No. Not at all. I'm a Clinical Educator."

This time he drew back. "A what?"

"Clinical Educator. I help people deal with ways to manage and prevent illness and help them with diets and other medical needs." She grinned. "But now that you asked, I guess I am a writer too. I also create and distribute brochures with health tips and information."

"Multi-talented then."

"I suppose you could say so, but..." She wrinkled her nose before she could stop herself. "I'm not so sure about the talent. I'm just blessed."

"Hmm? Blessed. I like that." Before he finished his last word, the horse let out a whinny and nudged forward.

"He's getting bored it looks like." Ally arched her eyebrow.

"She likes to cantor, and she won't take no for an answer."

"She?"

"Dixie is a mare." He shook his head. "I've known a few other women who won't take no for an answer." He chuckled before he finished the sentence.

His comment struck her. Was he were actually joking or reflecting his attitude. "Interesting." A sarcastic tone escaped her.

His expression faded to a frown. "I was only teasing. Male horses can be even more stubborn so it's just horses who want to exercise. I'm sorry if—"

She held up her hand. "No, I'm sorry. I should have

known you were joking. I'm a bit too aware of prejudices, I guess."

"No prejudice here. I like women." He jerked back. "Let me rephrase. I have great respect for women."

This time she couldn't control her laugh. "Goodness, we're both a bit edgy, aren't we?"

"Well, now that you mention it."

"I don't want to hold you up, but thanks for the lesson."

"Lesson?"

"Now I know Dixie's hair is sorrel, and…" She paused hoping he'd laugh. "it's the color of your hair too. Did you know that?"

A confused expression swept across his face until he relaxed and grinned. "No, I guess I didn't. I always call it medium brown."

"That's correct. But with hints of red."

He grinned and then broke into a laugh. "I'll have to look in a mirror when I get home. And your hair is wheat with hints of summer sun gold."

"Who's being a poet now?"

"Just speaking the truth, Miss." He glanced at her left hand. "It is Miss?"

Her lungs drained. "It is."

Another horse whinny followed by what she would call a mini-buck. "Okay, I think you're in trouble."

"No, that's Dixie's language. She wants to get moving." He grasped the reigns and gave her a wave. "Nice to meet you, but I have another woman here who's anxious to make progress."

She grinned. "Yes, I understand women. If they have plans in mind, they don't want to wait."

He gave her a wink. "I'll keep that in mind." He

flicked the reins, and he and Dixie trotted off.

She stepped back, unable to contain a laugh when something dawned on her. This was the first time in her life, she'd met a man and learned his horse's name, but not his. And yet this was a man whose name she would like to know.

♥

Dixie trotted up the hill while Cade Murphy's head spun. He'd been flirting, which he'd never done since he'd first met his wife. Since her startling death, he believed that love and marriage had been his gift from God along with their twins. He'd experienced that gift, and he would never need another. Chloe and Jolie kept his life on track. They'd been three when Janet died, and he'd raised them alone the past four years. He thought life was easier as the girls grew older, but he had a lot to learn.

As the thoughts rattled his brain, a new thought stabbed him. If Janet and the twins were the only gift he needed, then why was he flirting blatantly with a woman he'd just met. Met? He didn't even know her name.

Shaking the thought from his mind, he reached the base of Lee Mountain, paused a moment looking at the amazing landscape beyond, and then took a trail between the mountain's rise. Dixie trotted along, and he gazed out at the varying desert views and the rock formation.

Though he loved the rocky setting, his mind clogged with images of the mysterious, nameless woman, a woman who hadn't given a hint where she'd come from. All he knew was her career, a clinical educator, and her decision that his hair was sorrel. He rolled his eyes at his own lack of social graces. He should have introduced himself. She certainly would have responded.

Nudging the reins, he slowed Dixie, and as he did, his cell phone jingled. He drew her to a stop, and dug the phone out of his pocket, eyeing the caller. "Hi Mom. What's up? I hope the girls are fine."

A chuckle reached his ear. "Do I have to always bear bad news to call you?"

"No, but…you know me, Mom."

Silence met him a moment until she cleared her voice. "I know, Cade. I understand."

And she did. Since Janet's untimely death, phone calls sometimes struck him wrong. "So, as I said earlier, what's up?"

"The girls are having fun here, and they want to stay an extra week if you don't mind. They met some young gals about their age who are visiting their grandparents too, and those girls have invited them to some of their family events. If you say no, Cade, I understand. I'm sure you—"

"Yes, Mom, I miss them, but it's a long summer. I want them to have fun. I'm here with the horses and keeping up the ranch, so I haven't made fun plans for them. They're seven and I want them to enjoy themselves. It's fine, as long as you can put up with them."

"Cade! I adore those girls, and I—"

"Kidding, Mom. I know you adore the girls. So do I, but as I said, I want them to have a memorable summer. Here they can easily be bored." Another lesson learned, besides forgetting to introduce himself to someone he'd like to know and thus learn her name, he needed to stop making jokes that seemed to get him in trouble. "Are the girls there?"

"They're outside, but I can call them in and—"

"No, don't do that. I'm out on the mountain here with Dixie, and—"

"Dixie? Oh Cade, you mean you've met—"

"Dixie's a horse, Mom. I have to give them exercise, so I brought Dixie out for a ride."

"Oh…"

Her plaintive reaction pinged against his heart. "I'm not ready yet for much more than that."

"It's been four years, Cade. The girls could use a woman in their lives, and so could you, so I think…"

Silence, and he didn't break it.

"Cade, I'm sorry. Your dad often tells me to button my lip, and I guess I forget it has a button."

Though irked, he couldn't help but chuckle at her description. "Okay, Mom. I know you care about me and the girls. Maybe I'll call them in the morning—or I might even do Facetime with them, just to say hi. Tell them I love them."

"Okay, Son, and I'll let them know they can stay. I'm sure they'll be happy."

The call ended, but he continued to sit and stare into space while his mother's words revolved through his mind. "The girls could use a woman in their lives, and so could you." How did she know what he needed? He was doing fine, and so far, the girls seemed fine."

Or were they?

Dixie veered her head upward with a snort, and he took the hint. Females didn't have patience about waiting. They wanted what they wanted. He snapped the reins, and Dixie snorted and moved forward into an easy gait along the rocks.

His attitude slammed into his brain, and his eyes widened. What did he know about women? Other than Janet who'd lived for such a short time, he tried to make her happy even though he disliked her lack of patience at times. Still, he loved her and did his best to meet her needs.

For the past years, his familiarity was with fillies, not women. The weight of his negativity forced him to look at his pessimistic motivation. Avoidance. That was it if he faced the truth.

He flicked the reins sending Dixie into a canter, the easy rhythmic gait wrapped him in comfort, and yet motion didn't keep his mind from the golden blond woman. The nameless woman rattled him, but why?

He knew a few women. Not well, but he'd certainly spoken with some at church and in business. Women boarded their horses at his stable. They knew so much about the animals, giving him and most of the women something in common, but…

A deep blast of air shot from his lungs. He gazed at the scenery again which left him blank. Dixie had enough exercise, and he needed to get home and muck out the stable. Would Nameless enjoy that task? The question made him smile. He knew the answer. No one enjoyed that job, but mucking was part of owning horses. He slowed Dixie, reigned her around and headed back to the ranch.

As he approached the gate, he spotted something white stuck between the railing and the wire. Odd. Who would do business that way? He hadn't expected any of the horse owners or any visitors. When he accessed the gate, he reached down and tugged out the white envelope with no name or address. Rather than open it, he aimed Dixie for the corral.

After he removed the saddle and brushed her down, he gave her a goodbye nuzzle. "You were a good girl today, Dixie." He patted two others who moved closer, probably looking for a treat, but he had none to offer. Later he would have treats when he came out to muck the stable.

As he walked along the path to the house, he tore open the envelope and faltered. He squinted in the bright sunlight and paused to turn away so his shadow took the glare off the white paper and he could read her note.

It was nice meeting you today, and after I got back home, I began thinking of another experience I might enjoy. Though I've been on horseback a couple of times, I really know nothing about horses or being a true rider. I love new adventures, trying new things, so I wonder if you would have time to teach me more about horseback riding.

His heart jolted with the mystery woman's request for lessons. He glanced at the bottom of the page, relieved she was no longer a mystery. Allysa Grant. He closed his eyes picturing the attractive woman and putting her name to the image.

He raised his lids while her face embedded in his brain. He studied her neat script and finished the rest of her note.

I'm happy to pay you. I do work though as a Patient Educator, as I mentioned,

so I would need lessons later in the day or on my days off.

He reread the note and then gave it thought. So,

Allysa Grant wanted to learn riding. Why? She didn't own a horse, or she would have told him. She hadn't said much about herself except her employment. And now, she'd given a name. The wisdom of giving lessons to the woman, one who'd aroused his imagination for some meaning, didn't set well with him. He needed to concentrate on training horses, boarding them, and caring for them, and most important, raising his daughters. A woman that took his time didn't fall into that job description.

He would tell her no and suggest she try the Internet to find someone who taught horseback riding. He lifted his shoulders, having settled that problem, and trudged to the house. As soon as he opened the door, silence met him. Maybe he did miss his girls more than he admitted. He'd been raised to be independent and had enjoyed that role for years, but...

Lifting his shoulders, he ambled into the kitchen and opened the refrigerator for a soft drink. He grabbed a bottle of cola and turned toward the living room where he met more silence. After plopping into a chair, he sought the TV remote and turned it on, shifting channels until he found the news. Though he didn't really care to hear the news again since he'd listened to it earlier in the day, it was better than watching the middle of a soap opera or a mid-day movie. And no matter what, it broke the silence.

He leaned back and closed his eyes. The note crinkled as he relaxed, and he lifted his lids and set the envelope on the lamp table. She'd left a name but no phone number and no address so the burden was on her to get an answer. The answer was no. He said it over in his mind, but he didn't like saying no unless he had a significant reason.

As he thought about it, he did.

♥

After the third ring, Marcy finally picked up, and Ally had to muffle her chuckle, especially since she was out on the deck off her bedroom. Voices carried she'd learned to her embarrassment. "Hi stranger. You haven't returned my calls. Are you still angry because I didn't move to Cottonwood?

"Ally, you know why." Marcy released a lengthy breath. "Once again you want to drag me into your adventures…as you call them. To me, they're a pain in the rear, and you know it."

"I thought you were my best friend. You don't want me to experience fun things alone do you?"

"One more time, Ally. Your fun things are not fun to me. Hanging a mile up in the air on a plastic balloon in a wicker basket sounds like jumping out of a plane without a parachute. Who in the world wants to do that?"

"Me. But if you're that against it, maybe I can find someone else." The rancher's face rose in her thoughts. "So how about this? I'm planning to take horseback riding lessons. Now that's practical and fun too."

"Practical. Dear Lord, please tell me that I'm not hearing this."

"What?" Though she asked, she pictured Marcy's expression which meant she would now have to find logical reasons to prove it was practical.

"Practical? Did you buy a horse?"

"Well…no, but you never know. Think of how much fun it could be trotting along a mountain side and seeing all the beauty of—"

"Ally, the mountainside has already wiped out any thought of horseback riding even if I thought it might be fun. I think those people who ride mules down the Grand Canyon are on vacation from one of those 'Homes.'"

"Hey, now that you mentioned it, we're only two hours from the Grand Canyon. That would make riding lessons meaningful. Thanks for thinking of it."

"Oh, please. Count me out. No balloons, no horses, no mules. I value my life, and I'll stick to my comfy car and my two healthy legs. Both work well. My mouth works too, by the way. Want to have dinner together after work tomorrow?"

"Dinner?" Ally faltered. "In or out?"

"Huh?"

"Are you inviting me to eat at your house or going out to dinner?"

"Want to try a new restaurant? Now that's what's fun. And for you, it's an adventure."

"Hmm? Okay." She rolled her eyes. "Sure. Surprise me. I'll see you after work."

"Or maybe at work. See if you can get your lunch break at about eleven-thirty, and I can meet you in the cafeteria."

"I'll see what I can do. Be good, but then, with your quiet safe life, what else is there." She chuckled as she said goodbye, but noticed Marcy wasn't chuckling. She had to work on that woman and liven her life a little anyway. What's so dangerous about horseback riding? She pictured Marcy falling off a horse and breaking her arm or leg. Maybe she should shut up.

She leaned back against the lawn chair shuffling through her tasks for the day, but something caught her eye, and she looked up into the blue sky. Her chest tightened seeing a colorful hot air balloon drifting across the red rocks and heading up toward Lee Mountain.

Her urge to take a ride nudged her again. She had to phone one of the balloon companies, but first she needed to check on their requirements. She knew some went up with large baskets holding sixteen people or so. That's not what she wanted if she had a choice. She wanted a smaller basket, so she didn't have to vie for a view. She wasn't tall. At her last doctor's visit, she was only five feet-five inches. No wonder people joked about her being a shrimp.

Although she enjoyed sitting on her upper deck, she rose, shifted back the sliding door and step inside. She hurried through the bedroom and down the stairs to the little niche where she kept her computer.

Thirsty, she passed the desk and grabbed a soft drink and returned to her mini-office. Using the browser, she looked for a Sedona Hot Air Balloon Company with baskets for only six. She found one in only a moment—Northern Lights Balloon Expeditions. She read the information, gazed at the multitude of photographs and the more she looked, the more excited she became.

Though she preferred to go with someone, Marcy wouldn't be the person. Other people she knew from work marched through her mind, but no one had the kind of friendship with her as Marcy did. Maybe going alone would be better. She'd go without expectations.

Satisfied with the website information, she put the number into her phone, and hit call. The first try sounded a busy signal. She waited a few moments and tried again. This time it rang. When the man answered, she managed to collect her thoughts and organize the questions she had. Hearing the price, she choked. Though she assumed it wouldn't be inexpensive, she wasn't prepared for the amount he stated. She swallowed. "That's for one person?"

"Yes, Ma'am. The flight can be a few hours. Pilots burn a lot of fuel, and there's balloon upkeep plus the truck or van, plus the cost covers the pilot as well as the tracker."

"Tractor?"

"No, the tracker."

"Tracker, oh. I'm sorry." She was glad he couldn't see her face. "I've never been in a balloon before and…"

"No problem. The tracker is the person who is on the ground and follows the balloon in a four-wheeler with a trailer or a pick-up truck. At the end of the flight, the tracker helps to collect the balloon and basket and take it back to home base along with the passengers. That's a huge job."

"I can't imagine."

He chuckled. "I'm sure you can't. A balloon size can vary but it's often 80 feet high and about 50 feet circumference. Taller than most houses. Some of the larger ones are seven stories high. And they are very heavy. The basket is even heavier."

"Wow. I'm excited to take a ride. I hoped to bring a friend, but can I go alone?"

"You'll have the pilot and at least one other couple in the basket with you. Perhaps two, but there's still plenty of room."

"Okay, so when do you have an opening. It will

have to be a weekend, or I'll see if I can take a day off of work…or go in on a later shift."

"Let me check."

She waited, hearing background noises but nothing significant. Eventually he returned and listed openings he had. The weekends were booked for five weeks, and she gave her job thought and made a week day commitment. Now to get out of work for the day or shift with someone who worked the afternoon morning shift. "Do I send you a check or pay you when—"

"You'll need to send a check or stop by the office which ever is best."

She agreed, gave him her email address for future instructions, and ended the call, but not before she jotted down the time and date. Her arms prickled as the meaning of what she'd done lingered in her thoughts.

In less than a week, she would be floating through the air in a wicker basket a mile above the earth, and just as Marcy said, she'd be held there by a balloon filled with hot air from a burner. She'd read on line the gas jets are fueled by propane. Now all she needed to do is pray that nothing would go wrong.

Wrong. She meant to ask how they steer the balloons, but logic already sank in. The balloon floats on air so it goes where the wind blows. Landing had to be tricky. Did she want the details? She could check on the landing when she talked to a pilot. Or maybe not.

The next day after work, she met Marcy, and they went to one of the newer restaurants in Cottonwood, Black Bear Diner. She spotted the decorative black bear statues around the building on the outside and was surprised she'd never noticed them before.

Inside, she perused the menu, happy to see a

multitude of choices that sounded like home cooking—meatloaf, beef stew, chicken pot pie, and then she stopped and spotted her choice, hand-breaded chicken breast deep-fried, and golden brown served with mashed potatoes and vegetables. What more could a woman ask for?

The waitress came, and they ordered. Marcy chose fish and chips which sounded good too. Her decaf coffee arrived, and she took a swig of water before sipping the hot drink. She loved caffeine but in the evening, she drank decaf, if she wanted to sleep. Marcy drank milk of all things. She couldn't help but grin. "My balloon ride is in three days. I can't wait."

"So, you really did it."

She nodded. "When I spot something exciting, Marcy, I can't help myself."

"I know."

Marcy's sarcastic tone was meant for humor, but she didn't allow herself to even grin. "One day as life passes you by, you'll ask yourself why you missed so many things, and if you can't remember, ask me. I have the full list." Somehow, Marcy liked to get even, but instead of being irked, this time she chuckled.

Marcy didn't. "How's the horseback riding?"

"Nonexistent. I've focused on the balloon ride first." She took another sip of coffee. "But I'll get those lessons eventually."

"I never understand why, Ally, but then I don't have to. It's your crazy life, and I know you love it. What will you do when you get married and have kids. Will you still want—"

"Hold on, friend. Who said anything about marriage. Adventure and marriage don't go together unless I marry Indiana Jones. I hope you remember who—"

"I'm not stupid, Ally. Yes, I remember Harrison Ford in "Romancing the Stone," "Jewel of the Nile" and—"

"You don't have to sight the whole list. I believe you." The waitress arrived to her joy, and when she saw her order, her eyes widened. "How many people are supposed to eat this?" The huge platter overflowed with a pile of gold-brown chicken, a mound of mashed potatoes for a lumberjack and vegetables to last a week.

Marcy grinned. "I forgot to tell you. This place offers a bonus. You have enough food for a few days all at one cost."

"That savings will help pay for the cost of the balloon ride." Though she made a joke of it, the cost still rankled her, but then if she wanted fun and something different, as her mother once said, she had to pay the piper.

With the food on the table, they focused on eating and the reference to marriage and children had faded. Instead the conversation shifted to work, the luscious food, and vacation ideas for the summer. Once in a while, she and Marcy went together to a place for sightseeing, but again, that was it, no real excitement like zip-lining or white-water rafting. But still she was a faithful friend, and when she did agree to do something, she did it. So, no more complaining...at least for now. She bit her bottom lip to avoid a stupid grin.

Before she'd even put a dent in the amount of food on the plate, she slid it to the side. "I'll need a box. I can enjoy it tomorrow and maybe get a lunch too."

"And another dinner. I think husband and wives

could share this meal." Marcy grinned, letting her know she was forgiven for her sharp tongue about marriage, but she wasn't going to let it drop.

"No plans to marry, Marcy. Not one single thought or desire. I think marriage is wonderful for many people. You for example. Why aren't you seeking some nice guy who wants to have a family, and—"

"Let's not switch the subject, Ally. We were talking about you."

"But you shouldn't have been. That's my point."

"I don't understand why you're so adamant about marriage. First, I was only saying... Never mind. It's not important. But I really don't understand. Did your parents have a bad marriage?"

"Let's not get into that, okay? Right now, I'm happy with my life the way it is. I'm free and capable of surviving on my own. That's all I need right now. So, let's close the book on that story and talk about something else."

Marcy lifted both shoulders and released a long sigh. "Book closed."

Seeing her expression, Ally wished she'd let things slide and not make a big deal out of it. Her parents' relationship had nothing to do with her and especially not with anyone else. She had an okay relationship with both of them, and that's all she wanted.

Or was that all there was? They'd been a negative role model as far as relationships went, and she would lie if she said it didn't make a difference to her life. Though she wished it hadn't, if she were honest. Seeing two people miserable with so little to share, leading lives apart while living in the same house had made an impact on her. She wanted nothing to do with a life that dreadful. And yet they tried to keep it going. But why? Being unhappy had absolutely no charm for her.

♥

Ally glanced at her list of patients who needed help or input and headed down the hospital hallway. Often patients were ready to return home or to a facility, and she answered questions and reviewed their medication and health needs. She always filled out a form to send along with them and was available for calls.

Though she liked her work, especially knowing she was helping others, it had lost its excitement. She shook her head. At times she wished excitement wasn't her continual goal. How about enjoyment? Couldn't she just enjoy something rather than search for special moments to send her heart on a rollercoaster ride. That could mean life and death danger to a patient. She didn't want that. A puff of air escaped her as she trudged along the hallway, ready to face her next patient.

The clock ticked away the minutes and hours as her quitting time grew closer. She pictured the note she'd tucked into the rancher's gate and hoped it hadn't blow away. She'd heard nothing from him, and two days had passed already. Heard from him? How could she? Her heart sank. She'd only left her name. How stupid was that? He had no idea where she lived. And did she really care about learning to ride? Maybe. She'd ridden before, yet never knew if she were galloping, cantering, or trotting. Was there a difference?

Laughing at her stupidity, she gazed at the clock, pleased that she could say goodnight and head home. As she stepped outside, another situation plowed into her mind. After meeting the rancher, she'd totally forgotten about the hot air balloon ride. She hadn't contacted Marcy again, and Marcy certainly hadn't called her either. But then, she knew why. She could hear her friend moan. "No, not another adventure. Do you recall that I'm not adventurous?"

But why? Ally's forehead knit as she pictured cute and fun Marcy who'd avoided many fun things since she'd known her. One day she'd have to ask. Maybe then she'd understand. Everyone should have a little excitement yearning to come out.

Chapter 2

As the day for her balloon experience grew near, Ally had talked herself out of inviting anyone else to join her. With up to four more people in the basket, having her view blocked was not her goal. She wanted to see everything, even take photos, so five people and the pilot seemed plenty. And besides that, she'd done lots of things alone. Not everyone had her spirit.

In the back of her mind, she'd thought about the rancher she'd met and wondered if he'd been on a balloon ride but asking men for dates or even to accompany her on one of her ventures sat on her shelf of things she would never do. Apparently, she'd remained an old-fashioned girl. One who would expect a man to ask her out on a date. That's if she ever wanted a date a man.

Her pulse skipped again, as it did too often when she thought of Mr. Rancher. She longed to dismiss him from her mind. What made her think he'd be interested in hot air balloons or being part of one of her adventures? Still, he hung in her mind whether she wanted him to or not. She pictured his smile and those amazing sky-blue eyes. Her stomach tightened with the image.

Hold on there, Ally. You're heading for trouble. You're looking at something you've avoided always. Let it go.

Instead, she turned her mind to the morning. She'd arranged an actual day off from work, and in the morning…early in the morning, she would be waiting at the Village Mall where she would be picked up for the balloon ride. Her pulse skipped as it did with new experiences. Even though it was late spring and warm in the afternoon, mornings could be cool, so she'd spent time contemplating what to wear. Finally, she gave up. She'd dress for the warmer part of the day. She could brave a little chill and then, maybe the breeze would be perfect.

Before she forced her eyes to focus on the time in the dim light of early morning, a van pulled up. She eyed the logo on the side to make sure it was her ride. Prickled by a chill, she headed for the open door and climbed inside, aware that the chill may not have been the cold. Hanging in the sky in a wicker basket did seem truly a scary adventure. But she managed a smile. Excitement was her love.

"Good morning."

She responded to the driver and glanced at the other couple already in the seats behind her. "Is this your first balloon ride?"

The man shook his head. "It's my first. My wife had been on one years ago when she was a teen. I had hoped that would be enough for her, but…"

Ally chuckled. "Some of us can't get enough, I've learned." She grinned at the woman, and leaned back in the seat, gazing out the window at the silhouettes of the many red rock formations she could recognize in the daylight.

Her chill had passed, and the quiet, along with the rolling of the vehicle, lulled her into a haze. She closed her eyes, anticipating the experience to come. But to her surprise, a cool breeze washed over her and her eyes flew open. She opened her mouth to ask why they had stopped, but then she knew. They were there, and she'd fallen asleep. She hoped no one had noticed.

They climbed from the van and stood back watching the pilot and trackers, she suspected, move the huge bundle into the open area as well as the wicker basket. She eyed it, facing reality. These woven plants found in nature were going to be her floor where she'd stand a mile in the air. Was she nuts?

No. She refused to get nervous now. She'd done crazy things before and survived. She would have a wonderful time. Why did she have to question her decision today? As one of the men neared her, she decided to check her facts. "What are the baskets made from?"

"Rattan, cane, strong plant limbs that weave well and hold weight."

The tone of his voice made her wish she hadn't questioned him. "Thanks. I'm just curious."

Instead of asking anything else, she stood back and watched the flame from the propane tank heat the air as the balloon began to grow larger—larger than she had expected. Her confidence grew as the balloon began to rise and move above the wicker basket. She noticed that the lines were tied to keep it from lifting off.

With everything ready, the pilot called them to the basket. "Ballooning has traditions and it's time for your first. Before every ride, we stand together for the Balloonist's Prayer."

She glanced at the pilot to see if he would chuckle or wink, but he didn't. Instead he held a card in front of him, and she noticed the husband and wife joined hands and waited. She folded hers.

The pilot touched the wicker basket and read:

> *May the winds welcome you with softness.*
> *May the sun bless you with its warm hands.*
> *May you fly so high and so well*
> *that God has joined you in laughter*
> *and set you gently back again*
> *into the loving arms of Mother Earth.*

He backed away and motioned them to get into the basket while his words settled in her thoughts.

The couple climbed in first, and she followed. Before she suspected, the lines had been released, and the balloon began to rise into the air. They rose higher and higher in silence except for the sound from the propane jets. The van now looked like a toy, and the red rocks surrounding them jutted upward as if reaching for the basket, but the balloon rose higher as the breeze moved them along the vast landscape below.

Her first major sensation struck her. They were standing still, and yet she knew they weren't. They basket moved with the breeze though riders could feel nothing since they were moving at the same speed. Very different from riding in any other vehicle. Though it made sense, her senses struggled to accept the truth.

Resting her arms on the basket edge, she studied the long stretches of desert, thronged with cacti and scrub brush along with an occasional tree popping up. Such a diffcrent view from above. Her gaze drifted far ahead as distance grew between her and the earth below.

She turned toward the pilot. "How far up are we?"

"Just about a mile." He grinned. "What do you think?"

"I can't. I'm amazed and overwhelmed."

The woman sharing the ride chuckled. "I was too the first time I went up, and I'm still not much better. I tried to explain it to Bill, here, but I think he understands now."

Her husband gave her a playful poke. "I understand." He sent Ally a wink.

"By the way, my name is Barb." She stuck out her hand, and Ally grasped it.

"I'm Allysa but everyone calls me Ally."

"Nice to meet you, Ally."

"It is nice to fly with a couple others. I tried to finagle a friend to join me, but she thinks most of my ideas are over the top, so I gave up on her."

Barb nodded. "I almost gave up on Bill." She turned to him. "Didn't I."

He wobbled his head but didn't respond.

Ally sensed that Bill had lost tolerance for his wife's persistence. Wisdom should tell her that opening the family's business to a stranger wasn't going to heighten their relationship. Maybe that's why she'd avoided getting involved. Bad marriages or watching one go bad left her distrust of the "until death us do part" promise. And divorce wasn't anything she wanted to experience.

Trying not to be rude, she managed to give the couple a grin and turned the other way, again searching the landscape below. In the distance, she followed the line of large rocks, no longer the familiar formations she knew so well when she viewed them from the ground.

"You're looking down there at Cathedral Rock." The pilot pointed below, as if he'd read her mind.

"I wondered." She gave him a nod, noticing the scene below passed faster than it had earlier. The breeze must have picked up to an easy wind. She still felt nothing—no breeze, no motion, only stillness.

"How long are we up here?" She'd been the only one asking questions, and hoped they weren't irritating the others.

"It depends." The pilot grinned, but beneath the grin, she spotted an expression that aroused her curiosity.

An open ended comment never escaped her. "Depends on what?"

This time a frown met her before his answer did. "On finding a good spot to land especially when the wind picks up as it started doing a while ago."

"I thought we were moving faster." She'd noticed but hadn't been concerned. Maybe she should have. "I understand that we go where the wind goes."

"That's right." This time a less stressed look met her. "And if you look below, you see that we're in a vast area without streets or paths. It's desert, and our tracker has a more difficult time following us. He's my right arm in landing and helping me pack everything so we can get you back home. Not to say we won't. We will get you home, but right now, I have no idea when."

Ally's pulse skipped though she wanted to ease the stress. "This is a bonus, then. We're getting a longer ride than many people."

"Looks like it, but we must be down before sunset."

She jolted back again, picturing how she arrived at sunrise, and he was talking about sunset. A whole day in a wicker basket. And now he needs a place to land where his crew can reach him. She turned her attention to the landscape. The basket now headed for the large gray and red rocks that she suspected was Lee Mountain. She might spot her house, although it would be a mile below.

Again, images rose in her mind. Beyond the red rocks and bulky grey mountain, the balloon could sweep over neighborhoods of homes, her own included. Could it land on a small piece of property? She doubted it. So, what would they do? Her adventure had become more tenuous than anticipated. He'd already told them, they flew where the wind took them, so he had little choice as to move to the right or left or back up. His only choice was head up higher or go lower. And how would that help him find a place to land?

♥

The idea of fun had drifted away on the wind, and instead of adventure, the experience had multiplied to something more like danger. Though the pilot presented an air of confidence, she sensed that he had learned how to cover his apprehension. If he had learned that talent, today she needed lessons. Her mind flew as she glanced at the other couple who seemed to be unaware that they could be in danger.

"That's Lee Mountain, right?" She held her breath

as she pointed to the huge rocky mound in the distance.

"Yes, it is, and if we can get over that, the tracker can find us easily, so that's good news."

Good news? The word "if" caught her attention. "If we can get over..." What happened to the comfortable word "when?"

Approaching the mammoth grey rock, her heart picked up speed as forceful as the wind had done earlier. She closed her eyes, but then couldn't bare it and opened them again. The rough surface, deep gaps, and cave-like structures passed below them. The mountain looked as if it had grown since the last time she'd been there. Unending pylons of rock and crevices. As they drew closer, she finally understood. The basket had lowered greatly which meant they would have to land somewhere down there.

Time appeared to drag, and a gasp of pent up air ripped from her lungs when the view changed from the top of the mountain to the ground around it. Ahead she spotted homes, but in between a few opened fields greeted them like water to a thirsty man. Her hope rose as they floated forward and yet down. Lower and lower, until the view became familiar.

She spotted a house with a barn and what looked like a stable, surrounded by green grass and wheat colored fields. She shook her head. No, it couldn't be, but the closer they dropped, the surer she was. The home of the man she'd met on the horse, the Rancher that had clung to her thoughts for days since they'd met. No matter what she did to shake his image, she'd failed and why it happened left her confused. She'd never wanted a man nor needed one, so why allow one to linger in the thoughts?

Ah-ha, that was it. Horseback riding in the west. Another experience, another challenge. Her shoulders relaxed understanding her preoccupation with the rancher.

The pilot turned their way. "I need everyone to bend your knees, so you are ready for the impact of landing. Don't panic."

"Don't panic." No one wanted to hear that, but she'd heard. She clung to the wicker as they eased downward, while the flame that kept the air hot faded to a flicker, and the cool air carried them to earth. When the basket hit the ground with a heavy thud, she caught herself from falling and hurried to put her foot in one of the small openings to help the customers get out. But as she did, the basket tipped, and she struggled to keep herself from landing face first on the ground.

But ground sounded good to her after the danger she'd concocted in her head. The pilot had been right. No need to panic. He knew what he was doing, and she would have been smart to trust him. She had no need to panic.

When she gathered her wits and straightened up, she spotted a man heading their way. The tracker had made excellent time finding them. But as he drew closer, she'd been wrong. The man wasn't the tracker as her recognition sank in. He was her nameless rancher. He headed for the pilot and since he hadn't noticed her, she stayed back, embarrassed to find herself on his land.

They shook hands, and then he listened to the pilot's story of their difficulty finding a place to land. She took a step, but then revised her plan. Rather than break into their conversation, she could leave and walk home. That would be easier than waiting for the tracker and less hurtful than be snubbed by the rancher.

As she turned to explain her plan to the couple who'd been with her, she faltered and stood still. The pilot asked them to move in closer to him. Her heart skipped, again wanting to scream at the reaction she had around Mr. Rancher. She could only hope he didn't remember her.

"Everyone, I'd like you to meet the property owner whose land we used without permission, but who graciously said he was glad we landed safely." He gave Mr. Rancher a grin. "This is Cade Murphy, owner of this horse ranch, and we are all grateful."

They all nodded, although she tried to turn away from the rancher now with a name—Cade Murphy.

While she avoided looking his way, she noticed two men joining them, and in the driveway, she spotted the familiar truck with the logo.

"Ah, you found us." He turned to the group. "This is my crew everyone, and since you're here with the truck and our toast, I've also invited Mr. Murphy to—"

"Cade, please."

The pilot nodded. I've invited Cade to join us in our final traditions since he's been so very nice about our landing. First, we have our landing prayer.

> *The winds have welcomed you with softness.*
> *The sun had blessed you with its warm hands.*
> *You have flown so high and so well*
> *that God has joined you in laughter*
> *and set you gently back again*
> *into the loving arms of Mother Earth.*

"And now, the second part." The pilot reached

toward one of the crew members and grasped a bottle. "A champagne toast is also a tradition following our landing." He worked a moment on the cork until a loud pop came from the bottle, and foam rolled down the bottle neck.

One of the crew members handed him plastic glasses, and as he poured, the other tracker carried Champaign to each of them. As she grasped hers, she noticed that the no-longer-nameless rancher headed her way.

"Can I believe my eyes?" Eyes. She gazed at the sky-blue color of his, though harder to appreciate in the dimming light. "I dropped right out of heaven."

"I guess you did, and I'm glad."

Her pulse trotted up her arm. "Glad? Are you sure?"

"Positive."

Before he explained, the pilot gave the toast, and they all took a sip of the champagne. Though happy to be on the ground to toast their landing, she was more interested in hearing what his comment meant.

"So why are you glad?"

"I found an envelope on my fence with a request for riding lessons. I had only a bit of information. The note was from a woman named Allysa Grant. But what I didn't know is her address, a phone number or even an email address so…"

"Kind of dumb wasn't she?"

"Naw, just forgetful."

She had to stop herself from saying, "Now, how could I forget you." Instead, she found a safe topic. "How's Dixie? And that proves I'm not forgetful at all."

He shook his head with a grin. "I guess not. She's

fine. Would you like to say hello?"

Her legs wobbled as she fought back her reaction. She couldn't stand the ridiculous sensation that overcame her in his presence. Somehow, she'd become a middle school girl who had her first crush. "Certainly, but I have to excuse myself from the pilot so he knows where I'm going. I live too close to ride with them."

Cade stood back and waited while she talked to the pilot. He agreed and thanked her, but as she turned, he called her back. "Would you tell Cade I'd like to talk with him before he leaves."

"Sure will." She returned to Cade anxious to learn what that was about.

After she told Cade, she stayed back and let him go alone, not wanting to appear nosy even though she was. The conversation was short, including a hand shake, and he came back carrying a piece of paper. He waved it at her as he approached. "He gave me a gift."

A gift? I don't understand."

"Landings are usually on open land, he said, and not someone's property. But once in a while something happens, as it did today. I guess they have to land where they can find a spot. So, according to him, they always give the landowner a gift."

"Free dinner where?" She grinned.

"Nope. Sorry. A free hot air balloon ride for two."

"No." She grasped her chest, recalling that she'd paid more than two-hundred dollars for the ride. How could he give away a ride for two? "Do you know how much that's worth?"

Cade gazed at the paper and shrugged. "I have no idea."

"Guess."

He wrinkled his nose as if trying to smell the answer. "I'm a horrible guesser. How about one-hundred dollars?"

"How about five hundred dollars?"

"Five hundred what?" He stared at her with his mouth gaping.

"Dollars. Yes. Adventures cost money." She smiled and, for the first time, recognized that seeing him again was another adventure. "You'll love it and so will the friend you take along with you."

"That's right. It's a trip for two."

"It is. You'll have to tell me what you think." She shifted her focus to the stable. "So how 5about a visit with Dixie?"

His startled expression faded to a grin. "Right. You see what a gift can do to me, and one so expensive." He motioned for her to follow, and waved good bye to the others, as they headed for the stable.

The stable surprised her as they stepped inside where she'd expected to be blasted by the scent of manure, but the scent was fresh hay. Either Cade or an employee had to spend hours cleaning the stalls and adding fresh hay.

"This is lovely, Cade. It's so clean and fresh smelling."

"I board horses so it's important to keep it this way."

He stopped by one of the stalls and patted a brown-faced horse with a white streak along his nose. As she drew closer, she gaped at the multitude of white spots on his body. "What kind of horse is this? I've never seen one with polka dots."

He chuckled. "He's an appaloosa. We don't see a

lot of them around here, but they are great horses with a good temperament and they're strong."

She shifted to the stall and lifted her hand. "May I?"

"Sure." He stepped back as she moved in gliding her hand over the horse's nose. "You're a beautiful horse." She turned to Cade. "What's his name."

"Snickers. Besides the typical horse whinny, he adds a snicker sometimes."

She leaned even closer. "I'd love to hear that, but Snickers, I love your name." She turned back to Cade, astounded by the look on his face. "What are you thinking?"

"I wasn't expecting you to be a horse lover. You surprised me."

"I didn't know I was either, but how can a person not see the beauty. They're strong and bold, and yet gentle and sweet."

He lowered his head with a laugh. "When I'm working with one of these beauties that isn't behaving, I'll have to remember that. May I quote you. 'Strong and bold, and yet gentle and sweet.'"

"You may." She looked down the wall of stables and spotted the one she recognized. "Here you are." She darted past Cade and reached Dixie. "Hello, girl." She lifted her hand and patted her head. Dixie nuzzled her hand, and she recalled Cade's promise.

"Where's her treat? Remember, you said I—"

"Hold on." He shook his head but couldn't hide the grin sneaking to his lips.

His lips. Again, her heart did some kind of acrobatics. Cade returned and handed her a carrot.

"Here you go, Dixie." She held the carrot in her fingers as Dixie bobbed her head and grasped the carrot. "Was that nod a thank you?"

"It sure was."

Cade's earlier comment settled in her mind. He'd been surprised at her interest in horses, and in reality, so was she. She'd never known that horses were so interesting. They were like people. You never know until you meet them. And today she'd met Snickers and already knew Dixie. She was ready to meet a few more...but not today. After getting up before the sunrise, a tiredness swept her body and she was starving.

"I'd better let you get back to work, and I need to get home, but before I go, I think it would be smart to give you my phone number and my address. I live right up the road less than a mile from here."

He nodded and motioned toward the stable door. "Let's see if I can find paper and a pencil."

His comment made her grin, but also made her wonder. Was he one of those people where nothing has a place, so it was shoved anywhere? That would drive her crazy if...

If what? Air drained from her lungs. This was an adventure she had to end.

♥

After working since sunrise, Cade came in from the stable, his mind on two things—his twins and the neighbor who wanted to learn about horses. Talking with his girls came natural, so he plopped onto a kitchen chair and punched in his mother's phone number. It only rang once.

"Hello, Son. I see your face on my phone."

She tittered, and he still couldn't help but smile that his mother had a cell phone and a photo of him with his number. "I didn't call as soon as I planned. I suppose the girls are out playing. I should probably text first—"

"No need. Just hang on."

Although she tried to muffle the phone, he heard her clearly.

"Chloe. Jolie. Your daddy is on the phone."

He could hear their voices in the background, and he loved their reaction. He'd learned that which one of them could talk to him first was a life-long argument. He needed to share a solution to that problem.

"Daddy, hi. We're having so much fun."

He recognized Jolie's voice without a problem. "Hi Sweetheart. So, you've met some new girls at Grandma's, I hear."

"They're really fun, and we're all going to see a movie tomorrow in the afternoon."

"Great. I know Grandma loves having you there."

"But we miss you, Daddy."

"Jolie, I miss you and Chloe, too, but I want you to have fun. Here's an idea. So that I can talk with both of you, do you know how to turn Grandma's phone into a speaker phone?"

"Umm? Just a minute."

He waited while the three of them finally figured out what to do, and he laughed when all three voices burst from the speaker. "You did it. I can hear all of you."

Although he could hear them all, trying to sort out the conversation while even his mother added comments here and there, made him think about undoing the speaker part of it. "Slow down, ladies."

"Why Daddy? This is—"

"Chloe. Hi, my Sweet. I recognize your voice, but I

can't recognize three voices all blending into one. Do you understand?"

Silence. He could picture them all looking at each other until the truth struck them.

"You want us to talk separate?"

"That would help."

"Okay." Chloe's tone hinted at dejection.

"I love talking to all of you, but it's hard when everyone talks at once. If you take turns, I can hear each of you, and you can hear me. How's that?" He drew in a breath, hoping they understood.

"Okay." That was Jolie, he knew.

"So, you're having fun, and Grandma's loving your company. I miss you and look forward to seeing you in a week or so when you come back, but first I want you to have lots of fun, and take pictures so you can show me."

"We don't have a camera, Daddy." Chloe's concern made him smile. Her excuse gave him a good hint for their birthday gifts.

"But Grandma has a camera on her phone."

"She does?" Both girls pealed the words together.

"Mom, take a look at the screen of your phone. Do you see a logo called Camera?"

The mob dived into action, and soon he heard seven-year old squeals. "There Grandma, See it?"

"Cade, what do I do with it?"

"I'm sure the girls can help you figure it out, but hit the button and you'll see the screen turn into a camera. Then when you click the button at the bottom, it will take the picture, and you'll find it in the picture Gallery. That logo is there too."

"I think that's too much for my old mind, Cade."

"No it's not, but the girls will figure it out and then you'll be able to send me some photos or ask a teenage neighbor, one of them will fix you up."

"I can do that, Son."

"Good." With all the chaos he caused, he wished he'd kept his mouth shut. "Don't worry yourself, Mom. Girls you help Grandma and I'll look forward to seeing the photos. Have a wonderful time at Grandma's. I'm busy with the ranch so I'm doing fine. Love you all."

"Love you, too, Daddy."

He started to click off, but his mother snatched the phone as they girls' voices faded away, and he already knew what she would say. "Take care, Mom, and thanks for—"

"I'm fine, Son, but how about you? Wouldn't you enjoy a woman's touch? Someone to talk with in the evenings, not children, but a woman who shared your love of the ranch, and—"

"I enjoy the peace and quiet when evening comes, Mom. I can talk to the horses during the day, so don't you worry. I'm busy and not a bit bored. I love you, but I need to get moving, so you take care."

"But, Cade I…"

"Bye, Mom. Hugs and kisses." And he hung up as guilt rolled up his chest.

His tense shoulders hit the chair back, as he sat a moment staring into space. He loved his mother, but she had only one topic in mind, and it wasn't one he wanted to discuss. Maybe he should have told her about… No, that would give her hope. Poor Allysa would become a vision in his mother's eyes. But then, his neighbor seemed to have wheedled herself into his thoughts too often. And now she wanted to learn to horseback ride. A stream of air emptied his lungs. What was he in for now?

♥

Cade stared at the phone number Allysa had written on the piece of paper he'd found for her. He'd delayed a few days, asking himself one question after another and trying to make sense out of her request. The woman didn't even own a horse…although she did seem to like them…a lot.

An easy feeling rattled through him, and when he faced the truth, the feeling wasn't the problem. The woman was. He found nothing wrong with her, really, other than he found everything right. She truly seemed to like horses. She had a sense of humor. She radiated no desperation to find a man or someone to keep her safe. Instead, being unsafe—taking chances—seemed more her MO. Landing on his property in a hot air balloon validated her love of adventure. He almost wished he had a little adventure in his bones.

Instead he had twin seven-year old daughters who needed a father. He adored his girls even though at times his inadequacy struck him between the eyes. The girls needed a woman in their lives. His mother had pushed that in his face many times. Not that she wanted to hurt him or attack him, but that she loved him and the girls. She cared about their well-being.

He would never seek a woman to be his daughters' mother. If he had interest in a woman, his girls would be a major consideration, but as much would be her values, morals, faith, and how she helped him be the best husband and father that he could be. Janet had done that, and though she had been gone four years, what he'd learned had stayed with him. Still…

He sucked in air and forced himself to rise from the chair. Thinking accomplished nothing, and he'd already snubbed Allysa without really wanting to, but she confused him. Admit it, Cade. She caught his attention, and that was something he hadn't expected or wanted.

He'd had numerous single women from church, the rancher's organization, and even in the grocery store pursue him for reasons that made him cringe but later laugh. "Sir, can you tell me what you do with that vegetable?" He would look down at the summer squash and say, "Cook it." Her expression would usually sink, being aware that he didn't want to play her game. Rude. That's what he'd been, but he couldn't walk around with a sign on his back. "I'm not looking for a wife." He cringed with the thought.

Still, he'd gotten into a similar situation now. Instead of a vegetable, Allysa wanted to know how to ride a horse. Still "how tos" were "how tos," whether to cook a vegetable or ride a horse. He closed his eyes while her image filled his head. Lovely smile, amazing wheat colored hair washed in gold, and eyes that searched his as the green flecks winked in the soft brown color—hazel eyes, he'd heard them called.

What harm to teach her a few riding techniques? He'd taught his girls on ponies, but soon, they'd be ready for a gentle horse. His concern for entertaining the girls could fade when that happened. Horseback trips on the mountain paths that were safe. Riding to an open field for a picnic. Searching for Indian ruins that surrounded the red rock area. So many things.

The new thought spurred him on. He punched in her phone number and waited, but only a few seconds. Her pleasant "Hello" greeted his ear. "Hi, Allysa. This is Cade."

"Cade, I thought you lost the slip of paper." She released a faint titter. "I hope everything's okay."

"Top notch. I've just been busy. I spotted your note this morning so after working in the stables, I knew I'd better call before I did lose the paper."

"Thanks, and by the way. Please feel free to call me, Ally. That's the name friends and family call me, so…"

"Ally, it is. So, let me get down to business. Do you know your work schedule for this week or even next? Whatever works best for you."

"I have this Thursday and Friday off since I'm working the weekend."

"Sounds good. Which is best? Or do you want lessons both days."

"Both is fine with me unless I'm a natural." This time she chuckled. "I don't think we have to expect that though."

"Who knows?" He grinned, and his hesitation vanished. "How about coming here about nine or ten in the morning? Would that work?"

"Great. I'm up early."

"The horses are too, and they'll have been fed. It's a good time to work with them."

"Then we're on. I'll see you in two…oops…in a day. Thanks so much, and I do want to pay you for the lessons. I don't expect charity."

"No need to discuss that. We can talk when I see you."

"Okay, then. Thursday about nine."

"Right. I'll be there and so will the horses."

With a quick, "See you then," she hung up. He

stared at the phone, uncomfortable with the sensation of emptiness that swept through him at the silence. He bound up, stretched his arms over his head, and gazed out the window. Outside wasn't silent. At least, not with the horses. He headed for the door but then stopped. Ridiculous, the day he started to talk with horses, he needed serious help.

He'd hoped to laugh at the thought, but he couldn't. Without the girls and without a... Deal with it, Cade, old boy. This is your life. Enjoy it.

Chapter 3

Ally emptied her coffee cup, rinsed out her oatmeal bowl, and set them in the sink. She'd lowered her standards to instant oatmeal. Aware that making it from pure oats was best, today, she'd taken the easy way out. She'd promised Cade she'd be there at nine, and she would. She studied herself in the hall mirror from front and sides, hoping that jeans, a loose T-shirt, and her shoes that had a boot-look would be suitable.

At the last minute, she opened the hall closet and pulled out a straw hat with a little Western flair and plopped it on her head. She viewed her image again in the mirror and approved, though facing the fact that she had nothing else more appropriate. If she were going to get serious about this, she might need to spend a few dollars on proper attire—whatever that was.

Stepping into the morning air, a cool breeze rippled across her back. She paused questioning her decision to wear short sleeves, but the blue cloudiness sky answered her concern. In an hour or less, she would be warm, even hot.

With no need of a car, she started up the road, sensing her anxiousness by the wide strides she took up the steeper incline of the street. As the smaller home settings stood behind her, she could see the open stretch of land and soon the ranch. She paused at the gate, half expecting a note that said he had to do something else. No note appeared.

She unlatched the gate, stepped through, and hooked it again. No way did she want to be responsible for a horse escaping onto the open road. Ahead, she spotted Cade. He wore jeans and a dark shirt. When he noticed her, he came forward and she hurried to meet him.

"Good morning." She gave a wave as she approached. "The sky looks as if good weather is with us."

He nodded. "It does." He grinned. "I wondered if you might have second thoughts, but I see you haven't changed your mind."

"No, I'm ready." She pulled off the straw hat and took a playful bow. "If you knew me well, you'd know that I don't back away from new experiences. I call them adventures."

"Yes, you've told me, and I've seen it firsthand. You landed on my property in a hot air balloon, if you recall."

She chuckled. "I guess I did." The rough land roused in her memory. "And one day, you and someone will be doing the same on someone else's property. If you remember, you have two free rides coming to you."

"But I might be sixty before I use them. Actually, I could give them to you since you like wild and dangerous experiences."

"Wild and dangerous? Are you talking about a hot air balloon? It's thrilling. Can you imagine standing still in the air, yet knowing that you must be moving since the scenery changes, but you don't feel it? Can you imagine?"

"Not really, but I could survive life without feeling it."

"But you'd be cheated of something special."

He tilted his head. "Not to argue, but you have something special today."

"I do."

"Horseback riding. Become a real cowgirl. Learning the ropes. Understanding the terminology."

"Are you telling me there's that much to learn?"

"We'll start with learning the ropes. Getting on the saddle, communicating with the horse, experiencing the various types of gaits—walk, trot, canter and gallop. One more that's not as common is called the tölt or the running walk."

He grinned, and she rolled her eyes. "And I'm supposed to remember that?"

"You will with experience, but...I was just showing off a little."

She drew back, surprised as a hearty laugh broke from her chest. "I guess you succeeded."

"Maybe we should start again. Let's back up. First you need to meet Bliss."

"Bliss?"

"She's your horse, a quarter horse, one of the gentlest and easy going for the first lesson.

"I like the sound of that."

"I thought you might." He beckoned to her, and she joined him as they made their way to the stable.

Inside, a light reddish colored horse with a white streak down her nose stood waiting. Cade handed Ally a carrot, and she stood beside the stall with the treat in her hand and reached forward. Bliss gave a little nod, as Dixie had, that she liked to think it was a thank you as she took the carrot. The horse had to be a little over five feet tall, comparing her own height. She knew riders stuck their foot in the stirrup and threw their body onto the saddle. She must have done it before, but as she studied the situation, she had second thoughts.

"Are you ready?"

"Sure, if you have a ladder."

"A ladder?"

But before she could respond, he chuckled. "Ah, no, but I'm a great booster. I think that will work. You're more capable than you think."

"I'm glad someone has faith in me."

He slipped his arm around her shoulder and gave her a squeeze. A sensation rippled down her arms before she could control herself.

Cade let his arm drop. "Step back so I can open the stall."

She scooted backward, hoping to get a grip on her unwanted reaction to a friendly squeeze. Somehow, she needed to be in control before he helped her onto the saddle. Could she deal with that?

Instead, she turned her attention to the matter at hand and watched Cade bring the horse from the stall and attach the saddle. His professional attention to detail impressed her, but then, he had to know what he was doing. Confidence was an important factor of any career just as she was in her own.

Soon, Cade walked the horse out of the stable while she followed, asking herself over and over if she really wanted this much adventure. Yet the question made no sense. She'd been on a horse before—one of those dude ranches where no one expected the rider to be a champion. That's one thing she wasn't.

He handed her the reins. "Hang on while I get Dixie."

Dixie? She knew Dixie and would be more comfortable riding the friendly horse. She mulled the question over in her mind until Cade arrived riding the sorrel-colored Morgan. He slipped off while Dixie waited as if she knew her job.

"Cade, I'm familiar with Dixie. Would it make sense if I ride her? She knows me, and—"

He shook his head without letting her finish her sentence. "Dixie has a lot of spunk when she wants to, Ally. You'll be better off with Bliss for your first lesson. One day, you can ride Dixie."

How could she argue? She shut her mouth and moved to the stirrup, slipped in her right foot and then realized she'd made a big mistake. When she tried to pull her foot out, it caught on the boot. Bliss shifted as she grabbed for the saddle horn, but before she fell, Cade darted to her side and grabbed her waist and helped her down.

His laugh swept over her and she wanted to vanish with embarrassment. When he set her down, she spun around. "It wasn't funny."

"Sorry, but it was. I should have taken a video instead of grabbing you. It would have gone viral on the

Internet."

"So, I made a mistake." She knew he'd been teasing but she managed not to laugh. Instead she tilted her chin upward, wanting him to think she was irked.

"Two mistakes. First you used the wrong foot."

"Yes, I know. That's why I was trying to take my foot out of the stirrup."

"The second was not waiting for me to help you."

"I've been on a horse before." She pushed her fists into her waist.

"Did you climb on alone?"

"Well…not exactly."

"Ahh."

She drew back. "What does that mean?"

He shook his head and chucked her under her chin. "Put that chin down and be the Ally I know. Yes, you've been on a horse. Often, at dude ranches, they let you stand on a box to get your foot in the stirrup, and second you have a ranch hand by your side giving instructions and third—"

"I got it. I was showing off. Sorry."

He slipped his arm around her again. "Ally, you don't have to be sorry. I'm teasing you, but also pointing out that you can be hurt on a horse if you fall off or get tossed. This is one of your adventures. But I want this one to be both fun and safe. We move slowly, and then I'll give you the wildest horse I have, and you can show off."

"Thanks anyway." She'd heard him, but his arm distracted her to the point of desperation. What was there about this man that turned her into a gibbering teenager. She grasped for her adulthood. "Cade, I want to learn, and I get the point. Let's start over again. I'll wait for your help, and I'm sure by tomorrow, I'll have more working gray matter."

"It's working today, but backward." With another squeeze, he lowered his arm. "Let's give this another try."

This time she slipped her left foot into the stirrup, grabbed the horn, and with a slight boost from Cade, she landed on the saddle with everything intact. "How's that?"

"Perfect. Now grab the reins but hold on." He hurried back to Dixie and with one sweeping move, landed on the saddle with reins in his hand and walked to her side.

His body settled into the saddle as if he'd been born there—comfortable and in control. If only she could... But she couldn't. "Are we ready?"

"Before we start the lesson, I want you to look at how I'm holding the reins." He lifted his hand so she could see it. "Even the reins and move your hand up to about here." He demonstrated. "Hold the reins at that spot between the pinkie and index finger like this, and a firm thumb here." He demonstrated again, and she followed the instructions.

Though anxious to get started, Cade explained the whys and hows of communicating with the horse, and as she watched, she could only hope that she did half of his instructions correctly.

"Is this right?" She watched him check her hands and then drew back with his eyes on her position on the horse.

"Excellent. Keep your knees in that position but try to relax. Every movement is felt by Bliss and you can confuse her if you tighten up. Your foot in the stirrup is great. Not too deep but resting right where it is. Accidents can happen and if the foot is too deep in the stirrup and a rider falls, I don't want to see any broken bones or you being dragged."

The confidence she's clung to slipped from her grasp. "Now I'm not sure if I'm ready or not."

"You're ready." He gave her a wink. "Just a little movement of the rein, and Bliss will move forward or press your knee lightly forward."

She followed Cade's instructions, and Bliss understood her. The horse walked forward while Cade moved up and walked beside her. He motioned to the open field. "We'll head that way for now." She gave a quick nod while giving her body instructions to settle into the saddle, relax and move with the rhythm of the horse. To her surprise, by staying with the horse, she didn't feel those awful bumps she'd felt when she'd gone horseback riding at a dude ranch.

"You're looking good, Ally. We'll walk for a while, and then you can use a bit of knee pressure to signal her to trot. We'll save canter for another lesson."

His grin made her smile. "Good, I'd rather stay up here than land in that high grass."

"Good thinking."

Though the day had warmed, a soft breeze whispered through her hair. Bliss moved with ease, and she remained in the saddle where she wanted to be. Occasionally she remembered to straighten her back. Sitting up helped the horse understand what she wanted, and they both gained confidence.

"Let's try some turns." Cade leaned his shoulder to the right, and to her delight, Dixie's head followed, and she eased to the right.

Now if she could do that. She did the same, tilted her shoulder and looked to the right, and sure enough, Bliss followed. "Look at me."

Cade looked toward her and grinned. "A pro already. In a few moments we'll move left."

Her pulse skipped, hoping her action would result in the same. Once Cade shifted to the left, she followed his instructions, shoulder tilting left, and her eyes focused in that direction. Bliss remained straight. Trying to hide her fleeting frown, she repeated her action but this time she moved the rein slightly. Bliss turned left while she held back her cheer.

When she looked in the distance, Cade's home and out buildings appeared as a miniature, toy ranch setting. Her leg muscles had begun to ache, and she knew that was wrong. She'd tried to relax. Within moments of her awareness, Cade waved at her. She drew closer, hoping she hadn't done something wrong.

"I think you have it. You're doing so well it's time to trot."

Trot. He'd mentioned using her body as much as the reins, so she tightened her legs and gave a slight pressure forward. Bliss caught on and picked up speed, and though she'd gotten the feel of walking, the trot had lost its smoothness, and she found herself bouncing up and then smacking down on Bliss's back. That wasn't good for Bliss or her own backside.

"Cade?" She'd kept her voice soft and yet hoped he heard her. He hadn't. "Cade, I'm bouncing."

He heard her that time and shifted to her side. "Rock with the motion. If you follow the movement of the horse, you'll be more comfortable and so will Bliss."

"I know. I just… Okay, I'll figure it out. I suppose this is part of—"

"Part of that adventure you always want." He winked along with a grin and shifted away from her.

"Get into the motion. Relax. Keep the rhythm." Though it sounded easy, time passed before she caught on to the rhythm and began to enjoy the ride.

Though they'd traveled a distance from the ranch, their left turn carried them in a new direction and they drew closer to Lee Mountain. What excitement that could be to ride horseback into the mountains, but then, she would need experience and that wasn't today. She grinned at overzealous anticipation.

"Right turn."

Cade's direction met her ear, and she did what she'd done before with success. Maybe a horse begins to learn the rider. But changing directions while trotting had a whole different feel and she had to learn to relax and follow the rhythm. She let her focus settle on Cade's technique in the saddle. He looked as if he were born there with his back straight, his boots in the right spot on the stirrup and the reins perfect in his hands. He looked handsome, like a real western cowboy. Maybe one day his capable look and technique could be hers.

But she would need a lot more lessons. A lot more. The thought tightened her chest. Was it the riding she enjoyed, the idea of learning something new, or was it…the instructor who captured her interest. She hoped it was the adventure. She could handle that.

Cade held back until Ally trotted up beside him. "We need to slow before we get back. The horses need to cool down, and so we'll get back into the walking gait. Just loosen your knees, relax the reins, and see what happens."

Relaxing her knees was the hardest. For some reason, she thought her knees helped her stay on the horse. Yet at times, her balance seemed better when she did what he said and relaxed.

Bliss understood, and she gave the credit to Cade and Dixie who were walking beside her. But Cade gave her a nod, as if saying she'd done a good job, so she accepted it. The ranch drew nearer, but her gaze clung to the mightiness of Lee Mountain. The huge formation, with its blend of gray and sculptured red rocks jutting to the forefront, appeared as a high-rise backdrop towering above New York City or Chicago.

"I'd love to ride up there." She tilted her head in that direction.

"That's lesson thirty." He didn't grin this time.

"Really? I thought—"

"We'll see. It's hard on the horse but harder on the rider sometimes. You're doing great today, so be happy with that for now."

One thing she knew for sure. It took a lot to make her happy with herself. She wanted success and experience. Waiting had never been part of her unstable patience.

When she glanced back at Cade, his eyes were still directed to her. She gave a feeble nod, not wanting to get into a discussion while on horseback. And not really wanting to discuss it at all.

♥

Cade shifted his eyes from Ally. He could read from her expression and body language that she didn't want to wait for anything. She would learn. He could let her make her own decisions, but no way would he let her take responsibility. He could never do that. He loved his horses and he liked people, especially ones who listened to his wisdom. He'd worked with horses for years now. They'd become his friends—sadly, too true—and he had no plans to allow an overeager young woman or his I'll-teach-you attitude to take a chance on his horses or allow a determined someone to be injured.

He pushed his muddled thoughts aside and speculated the rest of his day. He'd spent too many days alone and perhaps he could... He stopped himself. Being alone had been fine. The girls would be back soon, and then he'd long for a little peace and quiet, even though he missed them when they were gone.

As they approached the stable, he didn't have to do much to Dixie. She turned and headed toward the comfort of home and the water trough. Bliss followed although he noticed that Ally had given the rein a faint pull to the right. She was learning.

He let Dixie drink as he slipped off her back and turned to Bliss. "This was a great first lesson, Ally." He drew Dixie's reins into his hands and hooked them on the saddle horn as Bliss headed for the trough.

"Ally, let me help you down." She'd already hooked the reins to the horn, and before he could give her a hand, she swung her leg over the horse before she grasped the saddle and clung to it.

He hurried to her side, put his arm around her waist, helped her slide to the ground. Her body melded to his, and his pulse skipped along his limbs and took away his breath. Her eyes met his, and he saw a flash of something that added heat to his pulse. He tried to relax his arms, but they wanted to stay wrapped around her. His reaction messed with his wisdom, and he struggled to untangle himself from the lovely young woman who hadn't moved. Finally, he found his voice.

"Okay, dismount will be part of lesson two." He managed a panicky grin.

She didn't smile. Instead, her expression appeared to be surprise or confusion. She cleared her throat. "Yes, I'll need to learn that tomorrow. I forgot how far down the ground is from the horse's back."

"Yoo!"

Cade's arms dropped as he heard the greeting. He turned, surprised to see his friend from Cottonwood. "Grif, what are you doing here? I had no idea I was going to be honored today." With Ally still wrapped in his arms, he gave her a squeeze and extended his hand to his friend. "I'm just finishing a riding lesson."

"So, you're stealing my business?" He grinned and grasped his hand. "I had a few things to do in Sedona, so I thought I'd stop and say hello. How's life?" His eyes shifted toward Ally while his mouth curved to a sly grin. "Pretty good, I would say."

"I'm just fine, Pal." He shifted around to catch Ally's attention and beckoned her to him. "Ally, this is a friend of mine from Cottonwood, Griffin Coleman. He owns a few horses with a riding stable and also owns a store that carries Western clothing and riding equipment."

She extended her hand. "Hi, Griffin. I might like to check out your clothing store if I become a real cowgirl."

Grif grasped her hand and held it. "It's Grif to friends, and if you're a cowgirl, you're definitely a friend."

She released his hand. "I'm not kidding about

clothes. I searched my closet this morning trying to find something that would be comfortable on a horse's back."

He lowered his gaze and eyed her from top to bottom. "Not bad, actually."

Cade's chest tightened. Though Grif's eyes were on him, he didn't hide the suggestive grin on his face.

Grif turned to Ally. "How long have you known, my good friend here?" He pointed his elbow toward Cade.

"About two days, if that."

"Really? I thought you looked rather chummy when I walked up."

Cade held up his hand. "That's called saving a young woman from falling off a horse. Dismount lessons are tomorrow."

Grif's eyebrows rose. "Hmm? Tomorrow. That's nice. Then you'll have three days under your belt." He let out a chuckle.

Cade's attempt to smile faded. "How about I finish my business here and then we can talk?"

"Sure." The coy look remained on Grif's face.

Shifting closer to Ally, Cade hoped to cover his irritation. He liked Grif and had never seen him so forward and outspoken. His reaction surprised him. "What time tomorrow, Ally?" He waited.

"The same time if that's good for you." Her eyes shifted from him to Grif.

"Perfect. Until tomorrow then. Oh yes, and thanks for your phone number and address."

She chuckled. "You're welcome. See you tomorrow morning." She gave a polite wave to Grif and headed toward the property gate and Jack's Canyon Road.

When she was out of earshot, Cade let his frown come to life. "What in the world was that about?"

"What?" Grif gave him a cockeyed look. "You surprised me, Pal."

"I surprised you?" Cade stepped back and eyed him top to bottom. "You looked like a playboy, the way you were ogling her."

"Whoa. You were the one with her in your arms, and I couldn't believe my eyes. You have women falling all over you, and you are hands off, but here you were with your arms around a very attractive young woman and you call me an ogler and a playboy? Hmm?"

Cade released a lengthy breath. "I'm sorry, Grif. I don't know what's gotten into me. I just felt—"

"Jealous." Grif grinned. "I understand. She's your woman and you want hands off."

"No, she's not my woman..." His stomach flipped, taking his breath away. "I only met her a couple days ago when we talked, and she expressed interest in learning how to ride horses." He shook his head and stopped. "Why am I explaining this to you?"

Grif shrugged. "You're protecting your interest, and don't be angry at me. I'm telling you Cade and I've told you before. Janet's death was heartbreaking. You were left not only without a wife, but with two tiny daughters to raise. You've done an amazing job, but it's time to live again."

"I do live. I have my girls and my horses and—"

"And what? No partner. No companion. No one to cuddle with at night. No one to turn to when you face problems. You're alone, Cade, and it's time you weren't."

"Grif, you sound like my mother."

"Smart woman." He gave Cade's arm a poke and then plopped his arm around his shoulders. "It's not my business, but you were a quality husband, a great father, and a wonderful friend. You're still two out of the three, but it's time, Cade."

"Listen. Who's talking. I've never met your wife. Why?"

Grif drew back and dropped his arm to his side. "I haven't found her yet."

"Maybe I haven't either. So, let's both back off and let what happens happen."

Grif shook his head and stared toward Lee Mountain. "Okay. My lips are sealed...for now."

"For good, I hope." Cade stuck out his hand and Grif gave it a firm shake. "Friends?"

"Absolutely. Who would I bug if I didn't have you?"

Cade released his grip and motioned to the house. "How about coming in for a soda or coffee?"

Grif nodded and followed him toward the house, while Cade's thoughts relived Grif's most startling comment. Jealous. Was he jealous? Did Grif have it right?

♥

Cade's friend continued to hang in Ally's mind throughout the day. His smug expression told her that he assumed they were a couple or that Cade was working on building a relationship. She wanted to laugh, but then it wasn't really funny. Grif had been more accurate than she wanted to admit. If Cade wasn't interested, she spent too much time fighting off the sensations that rattled her when he rose in her mind...which was too often.

In truth, she should avoid seeing Cade for a while. Yet, she had another riding lesson in the morning, and if she told him she couldn't make it, she would have to tell a lie as to why she cancelled. So, if she met the commitment, she could avoid seeing him after that.

Her shoulders lifted as she settled the plan in her mind, but then her shoulders drooped. She'd had fun with Cade so why did the fun have to stop? Fun had no relationship to romance or marriage. Fun was enjoyment, and she liked having a good time. Air escaped her lungs, and she came to a conclusion. Instead of worrying about it now, she would give it consideration after her next riding lesson. She had forever to decide then.

Rather than concentrating on her plan or lack of plan and Cade, she grasped her cell phone. She hadn't talked with Marcy in a couple of days, and though Marcy didn't like adventure, she did like to eat. She clicked on her phone number and waited.

Marcy picked up but before she could speak, Marcy did. "Hi, Ally. What's up?"

"Nothing's up, but I'm thinking about dinner. Want to come here and I can make something or I can introduce you to a good restaurant—Italian, Mexican, Thai, Chinese, whatever you're in the mood for."

"Hmm? You're tempting me, but first is this attached to a horseback or balloon ride, or a hike up a mountain or—"

"It's connected with eating. Nothing else."

"Then I accept. What time?" Marcy's tone had improved.

"How about now?"

"I'll be there in a half-hour. Will that work?"

Knowing Marcy, Ally could picture her eyeing her watch. "Sure will. See you then."

Ally clicked off and sank into her favorite chair. Marcy was a very attractive young woman, but she didn't appear to know it. If a guy came on to her, she assumed he was making fun. And no matter how often she had tried to convince Marcy, her friend didn't get it. At work, she'd noticed a couple of the single men eye Marcy and yet, Marcy pooh-poohed the attention as if it hadn't happened. Ally had given up.

If Marcy lived in Sedona, she would have opportunities to play a little matchmaking, but at this point, she still needed to recruit someone with Marcy in mind. Cade's friend Grif might be available, but then he might be married. She pushed the idea from her head and grinned at her silly attempts to line someone up for Marcy when she had no one waiting in line either.

Relationships had never fallen in line with her life purpose. She scuffed at the idea often, and yet at times thought of people she knew who were married and happy. It was possible. But then did she want to tie herself down to someone she had to please? Probably not. She liked being happy and pleasing Number One— herself. Being tangled up with someone meant making that person happy. Tossing the thought in her head, ignoring her own desires would be a difficult task for her. She'd never considered herself selfish, but did she border on that? A weight pressed against her eyebrows and she frowned.

After a moment, she drew in a breath, thinking of the fun she'd had with Cade. She liked his horses, but how long would that last? Having interest in something he liked wasn't selfish. It was good, so why chastise herself? No sin was attached to being true to oneself, so why had she questioned her actions? She stared at the ceiling, but not finding the answer there. she gave up. No reason came to mind.

Instead, she shifted her focus on which restaurant Marcy might enjoy. Many choices surrounded her, even a Moroccan Restaurant, Taste of Marrakech. Her mind slipped to the menu, recalling some of her favorite dishes. Lost in thought, her front door opened, and Marcy marched through. "Not much traffic so I made good time."

Marcy sank onto the sofa and grinned. "Okay, where are we going?"

"It's up to you." Though she said the words, her heart had settled on the Moroccan menu.

"Up to me?" Marcy rolled her eyes. "I don't think so. Tell me where we're going?"

Ally couldn't hold back a chuckle. "Do you like gyros?"

"You didn't mention Greek food. Why are you talking about gyros?"

"Do you like them?" She longed for one, but wanted Marcy to agree.

"They're okay. So, where's the Greek restaurant?"

Ally jumped up and flashed a grin. "I'll show you?"

Marcy remained seated, her expression shifted from speculation to a frown. "Okay, I know. I'm in for an adventure. Truly, Ally, I could wring your neck."

"Or you could thank me."

Marcy gave up and followed her outside.

With the restaurant close, in only a few minutes, Ally pulled up beside the Moroccan Restaurant, and guided Marcy toward the doorway.

But Marcy faltered and turned to her. "Taste of Marrakech? This isn't Greek,"

"You said Greek. I didn't." Ally moved ahead and beckoned her to follow.

Marcy gave a long sigh that she'd expected. Rolled eyes and sighs appeared to be a major method of conversation between her and Marcy.

As they stepped inside, Ally paused, noticing the inside seats were filled, but as she looked around, a table on the outside patio was available and they settled for that. The weather sun had shifted and a balmy breeze wafted around them.

Marcy settled back, her eyes shifting for views of the red rocks to the menu. "Organic, I see. That's for me. I'm having the beef stew and a side salad."

"Then we're ready. I'm getting the beef and lamb gyro with my favorite tzikiki sauce."

After placing their drink and food order, Ally leaned back, enjoying the breeze and memories of her time spent with Cade. Yes, she had to be in control, but still, she'd had a great time.

Marcy cleared her throat. "I don't want to interrupt but would you like to share?"

"Share?" She studied Marcy's face and then understood. "Sorry, I was thinking about the horseback riding lessons. You might enjoy them too, Marcy. It's really nice getting out and—"

"And waiting to be thrown off the horse or trampled beneath their hooves. No thanks. I'm not a sports enthusiast."

"You are so dramatic." Ally couldn't control her frown. "What you are is excellent at ruining someone else's fun."

"Then don't invite me along. How's that?"

Ally winced. Her remark had been rude. Guilt slithered down her back as she studied her friend's face. "Marcy, I'm sorry. I know you like your two feet on the ground and not anywhere near a rattlesnake."

"Correct. Safe and secure. Sensible and wise."

"And boring." Ally slapped her hand over her mouth too late. "Did you bring a muzzle?"

Marcy spurted a laugh. "No, but I will next time."

"Good." She pressed her lips together while wishing she had glue. "I promise, Marcy, that I will try to not be such a snarky person. We all have rights to be and do what we want, and I overstep the bounds too often."

"I'm glad you added you would 'try.'" Marcy grinned. "Now, tell me about your latest adventures. I know you're taking riding lessons."

"It's fun. I almost broke my leg trying to mount since my shoe jammed in the stirrup, but other than that I really love it."

"And what about the rancher?"

"I'm really attra...I really like him too. He's patient and knows a lot about horses. And guess what..."

"You've fallen in love and will be married soon."

Ally swung out her hand with a playful smack on Marcy's arm. "No. No marriage, and no falling anywhere except the bad mount. Although, Cade caught me."

"Superhero Cowboy caught you. Now that's very romantic."

She tried to hide her grin, but Grif's misjudged comment struck her unheeded. "Marcy, I have the perfect man for you. He's good at concocting misjudgments just as you are. He's a perfect match."

Marcy rolled her eyes again. "First I do not concoct misjudgments. And even more, I can't handle anything referenced perfect. You know that, and—"

Before she could finish her sentence, the waitress appeared with a tray holding their entrees and Marcy's salad. She set the food on the table and said she would return to refresh their drinks.

The break in conversation was a gift and with their focus on the food, the discussion ended. Relieved, Ally took a bite of the gyro and let out a sigh. She had enjoyed the dish every time she ate there, and Marcy seemed to enjoy her choices.

Though the sun lowered toward the horizon, a warm breeze remained. Their food vanished, and conversation returned, although different. Topics of marriage, horseback riding, and matchmaking had changed to their jobs. That seemed safer. But it didn't stop her thoughts. Grif was single, she hoped, and so was Marcy.

Chapter 4

The next day, Ally had awakened, anticipating the riding lesson. She'd had a crazy dream during the night that she and Cade had ridden up a huge mountain and couldn't find the path to get back. They were stranded there as the sun set and darkness covered them. The dream flickered in her thoughts in small bits and pieces, and as the details faded, the harder she tried to remember. Maybe it was best she didn't.

As she perused her closet to find something to wear, she wished she'd driven to Cottonwood to see what type of clothing Grif had in his store. Though her jeans worked the day before, she wanted to look the part just for the fun. After a quick search through her closet, she settled for her weathered jeans and found a blouse that looked somewhat like plaid.

All she really needed were the boots. Maybe she would pick up a pair for next time. Next time? Today her lessons ended. But did they have to? She really enjoyed getting to know more about horses and feeling a sense of progress communicating with the animal in a way they both understood what she wanted and then, occasionally she sensed that she knew what the horse wanted. The progress gave her a good feeling. One bordering on her love of a new journey.

Eyeing her bedroom alarm clock, she slipped on the boot-style shoes she'd worn the day before and hurried to the kitchen. She'd eaten a light breakfast, so she grabbed an apple and turned toward the door, but instead, she stopped. She hurried back and grabbed another smaller apple. She slipped one in a roomy shirt pocket and took a bite of the other as she headed up Jack's Canyon to Cade's ranch.

When she walked through the gate, she spotted Cade near the stable where he'd already saddled the horses. He gave her a wave, and she waved back though her interest was as much on which two horses had been saddled. She really wanted to ride Dixie, although Bliss had been a very gentle and obedient horse. For a new rider, she gave Bliss a thumb's up.

Today Cade had worn a real Western beige shirt with brown and blue stripes, a front and back yoke with buttoned double pockets, along with a Western-style straw hat, typical of real ranchers and cowboys. His broad shoulders and strong, solid appearance bubbled through her veins and warmed her chest. Within two days, she'd stepped into a Zane Grey novel and knotted with expectation.

"You look good." Cade stood, thumbs tucked into his pants pockets and eyed her. "Like that shirt. Today, you're a real cowgirl."

While gooseflesh raced along her limbs, she

managed to grin. "That will be proven if I can stay on the horse's back, mount and dismount without a broken arm or leg, and guide the horse where I want to go." She shrugged, and then drew back. "Oh, and keep my rear on the saddle without damaging it or the horse's back."

"It may take a few more lessons to get that good." He arched his brow and smiled.

"You mean you're willing to put up with me until I'm really good?"

"Hmm? Let's see. I suppose it depends on how many home cooked meals you're willing to payout for these lessons."

"Meals? What about those green backs?"

"Green backs are easy to come by, Miss. Home cooked meals are few and far between unless I cook them and then…" He lifted his broad shoulders in a playful shrug.

Her legs melted as she struggled to find her voice. "I'll have to see what I can do. Maybe I'm a fast learner."

"Then we'd better get started." He beckoned her to follow and she managed to keep up with him as he strode toward the two impatient horses. A few hoof strokes and a whinny gave away Dixie's impatience.

He'd saddled Bliss for her again, so she kept her mouth closed for once. Being responsible for her safety, Cade knew better than she did. He chose a horse who would keep her in one piece. As she walked toward Bliss, she reached in her pocket and pulled out the small apple. "Is this okay?"

He looked at her with question until he realized what she had. "Apple? Sure. Bliss will eat anything whether a carrot or an apple." His earlier frown had segued to a grin.

She held the apple in the palm of her hand, and Bliss needed no coaching to know what to do. She lifted it from her palm, flicked it deeper into her mouth and chewed.

"That was thoughtful, Ally. She'll be your friend for life."

The horse might but would Cade? She pressed her lips together, avoiding a comment and faced the saddle. Instead of reliving her embarrassment from the day before, she let Cade stand beside her while she slipped her left foot into the stirrup and managed to finagle her leg over the saddle to the other side.

Cade applauded and then tipped his hat. "Excellent." Happy with the compliment, his arm around her the day before slipped into her memory. Maybe she should have nearly fallen again. But with her earlier plan to be careful of getting involved, mounting the horse alone covered her new resolve.

Cade stepped past her, mounted Dixie and appeared beside her. "Should we review, or do you want to try on your own."

"On my own." Wisdom dueled with her determination. "I've been going over the steps in my head." Sort of…

Cade gave a signal, and Dixie followed his lead while she maneuvered the reins around as she'd been taught and added the forward pressure. Bliss caught on to her relief and headed down the path behind Dixie. A good feeling swept through her. Maybe she could be a satisfactory rider one day.

Dixie moved ahead, and she noted her gait had

changed. Time to move from a walk to a trot. Though she tried to catch up with Cade, Bliss continued to trot further behind them. Hoping she might trot a little faster, she tightened her knees and leaned an inch forward. Bliss caught on and in moments, she was trotting next to Cade.

Enjoying the experience beside him, she found focusing on the ride became overshadowed by her desire to talk. She had questions and plain old curiosity. "If I have to cook, what's your favorite food?"

He flashed her a look. "I like food. Surprise me. Make one of your favorite dishes. I'll enjoy that."

"What if it's snails?"

He drew back and then eyed her. "Really?"

"No, but I was just checking." She chuckled. "If you're willing to eat what I cook, then I will surprise you."

"As I said, I like surprises." He smiled, and she studied his even white teeth, surrounded by full pink lips that made her pulse gallop. She'd never had the experience on a horse but sometimes when gazing at Cade, she experienced her heart taking flight.

She closed her mouth, enjoying the feel of a soft breeze whispering through her hair. Without conversation, she focused on the landscape and congratulated herself that she'd somehow captured Bliss's rhythm so she'd remained in the saddle without the aching bumps.

Cade shifted in a new direction, and Bliss followed her command without incident. They headed deeper into the desert, and as the sun rose higher, she wished she'd thought to bring a hat, both to shade her eyes and cover her head from sunburn.

Bliss trotted along while she sat with pride, knowing she'd communicated with her and also understood the need to move with her rhythm. Cade glanced her way with a grin, and her heart did another pinwheel twirl. Her emotions were out of control.

"Ready to learn the gallop?"

"Really?" She studied his expression to understand if he were teasing.

"Really. Why not? You're trotting like a pro."

She pressed her lips together to stop from verbally questioning his honesty. "You think I can?"

"The important question is are you ready? Do you feel confident with the trot?"

"I do." Excitement slithered through her limbs. "I'm more interested in your confidence in me."

"I wouldn't ask you if I thought you would fail. I'm a joker at times, but not when it comes to harming you or the horse."

She should have known. She dragged in a breath, letting his reasoning sweep through her mind. "I'd like to try. If I become scared or uncomfortable, I'll let you know."

"Okay. Then watch what I do and do the same."

She kept her gaze glued to Cade's actions with the horse, the shift in his body weight, the movement of his legs and the reins. She kept the order straight in her mind and followed his actions. Already in a canter, she shifted forward in the saddle and pressed her legs forward. Bliss picked up pace and the horse's gait swept into a gallop. Her hands rested on the reins, so a slight movement could slow her down along with sitting back in the saddle.

Cade let out a "yahoo" as she bounded beside him.

They rode side by side while she could barely believe she had accomplished so much with Cade as her teacher. He gave her a signal, and she leaned back without the use of reins and felt Bliss slowing back into a canter.

Cade gave her a thumbs up, and then reversed the direction back towards the ranch. Her heart soared with the joy of riding and doing it with a real rancher cowboy, and the feeling lingered.

When they returned to the stable, she managed to dismount without a mistake. Cade sauntered to Bliss's side. "Great job today, Ally. You're becoming a real cowgirl."

Becoming? "Thanks for that huge vote of confidence, but I know I have more to learn, and—" She motioned to her old jeans and sort of plaid blouse—"I think I should visit Grif's Western store and pick up a few items if I'm going to be serious."

"Here's my advice." He lifted his hat. "You need one of these…woman's versions though."

"It's on my list. I fear I'll get a sunburn on my head."

"We don't want any hotheads around here, so I'm glad you recognize the hat's not just to make you look like a cowgirl, but to be a healthy one."

She managed a grin along with a fleeting nod. Too many other things slipped into her mind. "I'm wondering if you have time for a few more lessons so I can do some mountain riding with one of the horses. You remember I love—"

"Adventure. How could I forget?"

She waited, hoping that he'd answer without more probing.

He remained silent for a time as he became involved removing the horses' saddles and other tack. She moved closer and watched his technique and then began removing Bliss's tack as well.

"Ally, you don't have to do this, you know. I can handle it…unless you want to learn more."

She drew in a breath, struggling with what it was she wanted. "Yes, I'd like to learn more about horses and become a better rider."

"Right now, I have more time than usual, Ally, so I can continue with the lessons if you really want to learn more. I'm not sure you need to know everything unless you're considering buying a horse."

His strange expression made her question what he meant. "I'm not sure what the future holds, but if I decide to own one, it would be nice to learn from the authority." A slight curve of his mouth clued her that he was trying not to smile. "And I know where I could board the horse if I did buy one."

"Really. You need to check the place out and make sure it has a business license and complies to the state regulations. That helps you makes sure the owner of the stable has experience and has the facilities needed for the horses' health and well-being."

"Goodness, I had no idea, but then I trust the man who owns the only stable I would consider. Maybe you know him. His name is Cade Murphy."

"He's a crook, I think. I'd beware."

She slipped her arm around his shoulder. "You're prejudice. I think he's a great guy, and in fact, I meant to invite him to dinner tonight as payment for his excellent lessons."

"Tonight? Hmm? I'm guessing that he might be

available. Is available. That's how sure I am."

"Great, and maybe he and I can talk more about future lessons, and…" She stumbled over the "and." And what? The idea of a future with Cade stumbled into her mind, and that scared her.

She loved freedom and fun. She could come and go as she wanted with nothing to tie her down. Not a husband or a family. She'd never been a woman who thought about having kids.

The idea left her confused. Kids were, perhaps, a legacy, but what might her legacy be, a positive gift to leave behind when they are gone. But that meant focusing on the legacy and not on the moment. She's always loved the moment. What came next gave her the adventure.

"And?" Cade's voice jarred her thoughts. Flustered, she jerked herself back to the moment. "Sorry. Thinking of the future, I started to dig into my head about what I really wanted to learn and do. I was off in another world."

"So, what is it you want for the future?" His gaze clung to hers.

The blue of his eyes sent her on a wavy sea heading somewhere unknown. Her pulse billowed through her chest and bobbed on the edge of nowhere. She dragged in air. "I have no idea. Things just happen. That's how we met. A fluke of happening. A moment in time with a hook."

"Hmm? A hook. Since I'm part of that moment in time, I'd like to know about the hook."

Why had she used the term hook? "Maybe not a hook exactly but an opportunity to learn something new."

"Then you've succeeded. Congratulations." He gave her a royal bow.

Feeling giddy, she curtsied. "So how about dinner?"

"That sounds nice. One of these days, I'll be tied up and not able to accept."

His expression plus the warning weighted her chest. "I hope not forever."

♥

Forever. Cade frozen to the spot. He'd been flirting with Ally, something he never did, and yet he'd never mentioned the twins. He'd only indicated he'd soon be busy. Why didn't he just tell her? He studied her face, now filled with question. More like concern. This wasn't the time to break the news, and he needed to say something. "I can work things out sometimes."

Her expression softened. Though no smile, she looked at ease. "I'd better get going if you're coming for dinner. Is there anything you can't or don't eat?"

"Snake. Javelina. Oh, and snails."

A smile blossomed into sunshine. "I think you're safe. I just ran out of snake meat and I'm not a fan of snails either."

"Glad to hear it. What time would you like me to arrive?"

"Anytime, I'll have dinner ready about five or so."

"Okay, I'll see you then." He tipped his hat, and as he set it back on his head, another thought came to mind. "And listen, if you want to go to Grif's store, I'm heading there tomorrow. You're welcome to join me if you'd like."

She paused a moment before her head bobbed. "Perfect. That'll save my getting lost. I should know Cottonwood since my friend Marcy lives there and I work there. At least I know how to get to work."

"Congratulations. After tomorrow, you'll know how to get to Grif's"

She chuckled and spun around. "And then I'll have my hat. No more hot head."

He tousled her hair and then stood there with his head in a whirr. That was far too familiar, but she only laughed so he pardoned himself and made a promise to himself he wouldn't do that again.

Sometimes promises weren't kept. That was his problem.

Ally gave a wave and headed toward the gate while he watched her go, finding himself more confused than ever. First, he loved his girls and he'd never mentioned them to her. Why? But it didn't take long to answer his own question. Ally wanted freedom, excitement, adventure. Having two young daughters put a kibosh on that style of living.

Thinking of the girls, he finished up the work with the horses and headed for the house. He wanted to check with Grandma and make sure all was well and if the girls were ready to come home. Tonight, he should say something about them to Ally, and yet what did it matter?

Once inside, he settled into his favorite chair, leaned back and raised his feet. He closed his eyes, thinking about the day and all that had happened. As much as he cautioned himself, Ally attached to his mind like the girl's favorite stickers. Bright, fun and different. He tugged his phone from his shirt pocket and hit his mother's number. It took a moment and when he heard the voice, he knew what had happened.

"Hi Chloe. Grandma let you answer, I suspect."

Chloe giggled. "We saw your picture on Grandma's phone, so she knew it was you, Daddy."

"That's nice of Grandma to have my picture there."

"That way she knows it's you calling. If it's someone else, we can't answer."

Ah, smart Mom. "How's Jolie doing? Is she there?"

"She's in the kitchen sneaking one of Grandma's cookies that she baked."

"Sneaking a cookie, huh?"

"Yep, but Grandma said I could have one too. She made them for the church bake sale, but she told us we could have a couple."

He couldn't help but chuckle. "Let me talk to Grandma."

"Okay."

He listened to the handoff, with Jolie yelling in the background that she didn't get a chance to talk, and his poor mother was trying to console her with the promise she could talk before she hung up. "Hi, Son. I suppose you can hear the—"

"Whining. Yes, I can. Tell Jolie to eat her cookie and I'll talk to her shortly."

Once the message was delivered, he got down to business. "Mom, how much longer can you deal with those girls? I'm thinking it's time to give you a break."

"Well now, I promised them that we can go the church picnic on Sunday so how about we bring them back on Monday. Would that work?"

"Mom, I can drive there and pick them—"

"No need. We want to come since we're going to do a few things in Sedona anyway."

"Okay, then. I'll be here waiting on Monday. And put Jolie on the phone before I hang up or she'll go into a tizzy."

His Mom chuckled and put Jolie on the phone.

"Hi Daddy, we're coming home next week."

"I know Sweetie. Have fun at the picnic and I'll see you at home Monday. I love you."

"Love you, too, Daddy."

Hearing silence, he clicked off and set the phone on the table while his mind whirled. His life was getting back to normal very soon, but sadly, he'd begun to enjoy the new things going on in his life. Ally had added a bit of excitement to his life, something he never thought he would enjoy again with a woman other than Janet. With the girls returning home, he would have to learn to blend the old with the new…unless Ally turned her back on him. His shoulders lowered as the thought settled in his mind. She'd been very blunt about having her freedom. She could give up the lessons and him. She could say goodbye and walk away.

♥

Ally searched the refrigerator and came up with enough to make dinner. If her arm were long enough, she'd pat herself on the back. Grateful she'd taken out chicken from the freezer for dinner that evening, she found it thawed enough while sitting in the fridge, and she'd located a can of cream of chicken soup. One of her easy to make recipes struck her when she saw the thawing chicken, so she'd make Cade one of her favorite meals.

The more time she spent with him, the more she seemed drawn to his ways. He had a nice personality, very patient with her for sure, and thoughtful. She liked his easy-going sense of humor and on top of it all, he was very good-looking. But as those thoughts struck her, she had to ask herself the same question. Did she want to be tied down with another person in her life? Would he enjoy the crazy things she liked to do?

The question knocked her cold. Why ask those questions? He'd given her no signs that he had any interest in her other than to teach her horseback riding and a little info about raising horses.

And on top of it, she'd just reminded herself a relationship with a man had never been on her bucket list. Not on any list. She'd avoided getting involved. Thankfully Marcy had put up with her and she had a solid friendship with Marcy who was also patient and direct. She liked that. Marcy said what she thought so no games entered their friendship. Ally knew where she stood with Marcy.

As she worked on the meal, she managed to clear her head, reiterating her joys in life, learning new things, enjoying excitement and adventure, being a good person to others, being honest and hanging on to her faith. What more did she need?

When she gazed at the clock, she needed to get going on the meal or Cade would arrive while she was still reiterating her joys in life. Chuckling at herself, she delved into the recipe and lined up the ingredients. Anything missing wouldn't be a problem since she was good at improvising.

After sliding the casserole into the oven, she checked on salad ingredients and found lettuce, plum tomatoes, green onions and a yellow pepper. Perfect. As she tugged leaves from the head of lettuce, the doorbell rang. Her heart skipped to her throat, and she took a moment to regain her wits and head for the door.

When she opened it, Cade stood there dressed in a

different shirt and pants, not jeans. She'd never seen him in apparel that wasn't western. "Come in." She opened the door wider after standing there a moment gawking. "Can I get you something to drink? Soda? Lemonade? Water? Coffee?"

Cade muffled an obvious laugh and followed her across the room. "How about lemonade? I haven't had any for a while and I like it."

"Great." She motioned to the sofa and then a chair. "Have a seat and I'll be right back."

She hurried into the kitchen, added ice to a glass and poured the lemonade, and then grabbed another glass and poured some for herself. She eyed the beginnings of the salad and faced her mistake but grabbed the lemonade and returned to the living room.

"Here you go, and Cade, I forgot. I'm making a salad and you can stay here or if you want, you can sit in the kitchen with me until I get that job done."

He stood and tilted his head toward the kitchen. "I'll join you if you don't mind."

"Not at all." She beckoned him to follow and she returned with the handsome man behind her. She didn't have to offer him a seat. Cade pulled out a chair and sat at the table.

"Something smells delicious?"

"Thanks, it's one of my favorite casseroles. I hope you like chicken."

"I do. I'm not too fussy if you recall."

She did. She grinned recalling their silly conversation on what he liked and a couple things he didn't like. "I promise. You wouldn't find even one snail in anything."

He shook his head as he smiled. "I feel so much

better…safer really."

She tried to concentrate on the salad, but her gaze kept drifting to Cade as he watched her every move as if he'd never made a salad. "I'm done." She lifted the salad bowl and set it in the fridge before rinsing off the cutting board and knife. "Let's be comfortable."

She tilted her head toward the kitchen door.

He rose and walked ahead of her, settling into the same chair he'd been in earlier while she sat on the sofa across from him. "Dinner will be a few more minutes." She eyed her watch. "Probably a half hour. I guess I took longer than I meant to."

"Are you in a rush?" His brow arched as he studied her.

"Not at all, but I thought you might be."

"Not now. Horses are bedded down for the evening. I don't have to cook a meal or sneak out and buy fast food, so I'm good."

"Tell me about yourself, Cade. How long have you lived here? Did you own horses somewhere else?"

His grin grew wider as she tossed out one question after another without realizing it until she saw his expression. "I could have stopped with the first question. Right?"

"Right, but then would that be the Ally that we all know and love?" He again grinned but his lips looked forced. Was it the word love that had upset him? It had surprised her.

"I suppose not. And I'm rather surprised you know me so well for such a short friendship…association…whatever it is."

"By now, it's a friendship, Ally. You've added some fun to my life."

"Thank you, and I think of you as a friend too. I love learning about the horses. At first it was for the excitement of becoming a better rider, but now I'm appreciating so many things about, not only riding, but raising horses. It's almost harder than raising a family."

He shrugged. "I doubt that, but…"

His expression had altered when she said family, and her curiosity rose. "Were you married once, Cade? Or maybe you still are?"

"I was married for a short time. My wife died suddenly from a disease no one knew she had. It was a shock to everyone. She's been gone for four years, so I've learned to be a bachelor again."

"I'm so sorry, Cade. I shouldn't have asked."

One day she wanted to learn when questions should not be asked. Losing his wife in such a short time. His biggest blessing was having no children.

"It's fine, Ally. I assume you've never married."

"Correct. Marriage is…" She struggled to continue as a ragged breath tore from her throat. "I didn't grow up with a good role model for marriage. My parents stayed together but instead of a marriage made in heaven, I think theirs was one made in hell. They had nothing in common. I don't understand why they married. I was born more than a year after their wedding, so it wasn't me. I asked myself for a long time if my mom was pregnant. Apparently, she wasn't when I used my head."

"A bad marriage can be gruesome. I often question why they happen too, but we all know they do. People think they can change people, but they can't, or they haven't been open about who they really are when it comes to living life day in and day out. Spending time on dates isn't a good picture of life when married."

"That's what I've always feared. Comparing a relationship to what I saw with my parents can give a person hints, but as you said, daily interaction can bring the snakes out of the closet."

"Snakes? Interesting comparison."

"Maybe I should have said truth. That's what we're talking about."

"Yes, it is. Truth is necessary for marriage. Communication, honesty, and faith."

"Faith. I agree with you so much. I'm not the best church goer, but I do have faith and try to follow the commandments as best I can."

He nodded. "That's all the Lord expects. We do our best to be His child in the world."

"I like that." As the words left her mouth, the buzzer went off in the kitchen. "Hear that? It's dinner time."

♥

"Would you like some more, Cade? Just help yourself." His belt had already tightened around his waist, but he was tempted. "This is really great, but I fear I might blow up."

She grinned at his silliness but understood. "I don't want you to blow up. Where would I get my riding lessons? And to be honest, I'm stuffed too, so I understand."

"Hmm?" He tilted his head with a sly grin. "Then we have more in common than I imagined."

Not sure she totally understood, she managed a head nod, while his comment swept through her like a whirlwind. She liked the idea of having something in common with Cade, but she wanted to hear what he thought they had in common. "What…?" Her tongue tangled with a question she didn't want to ask. Instead she flipped the topic. "What time would you want to go to Cottonwood? You mentioned showing me Grif's store."

"I did. Early afternoon would be good. I need to pick up a few groceries and I can check on a few items I want to get at Grif's store too."

"Groceries? Sounds good. I'll make a short list. I do need a few things."

He didn't respond and appeared to be preoccupied. Instead of breaking the silence, she waited a moment hoping he'd say something. Another minute passed before he focused on her.

"Sorry. I have a few things on my mind, and I realize if we go to Cottonwood, we'll need to either cancel your lesson or make it very early."

Though disappointed, she eyed the stress appearing on his face and gave the answer she should, whether it was what she wanted or not. "That's fine. We can arrange it for another time."

"Thanks, I…" He glanced away, his jaw shifting as if he had words stuck in his throat. "We'll work something out. And though I enjoyed the meal and conversation, I have some things to take care of tonight, so I think I'll get going. I hope that's okay."

"Certainly. I just owed you a dinner."

"That was only a joke, but I did enjoy it. Thanks again, and I'll see you tomorrow then around noon. Is that good?"

"It's great. We should be back in time…" He frowned. "In time for me to take care of some business."

Business? Something was wrong, but she shut her mouth and didn't ask.

♥

Cade struggled with himself for the rest of the evening and woke with the same horrible scuffle tossing in his mind. Why hadn't he been honest? He had the opportunity to mention the twins. He loved his girls...adored them, so why would he not mention them...not tell Ally that he had two daughters who would be home in the afternoon.

Ally would know soon, and if he were in her shoes, he would question why she hadn't mentioned his children. What did he think would happen? What if...? He slumped against the chair, ashamed and guilt-ridden. "Lord, forgive me."

How much longer could he try to pretend like Ally's connection to him was riding lessons? That's how he met her, but they'd already admitted they were friends. Would she run away if she realized he had children. Her fun, adventure, excitement mantra clung in his thoughts, but if that's all life was to her, their friendship wouldn't last. It couldn't last. Excitement and adventure wasn't what made a relationship. Trust, kindness and love did.

Tears welled in his eyes as he tugged his handkerchief from his back pocket and wiped away the moisture running down his cheeks. He hadn't shed tears for a couple of years when he finally managed to deal with Janet's death. But what kind of a father was he? The girls should be the most important thing in his life, not trying to impress a woman that he wasn't even sure...

Sure of what? His shoulders lowered again. Yes, he

liked Ally. He liked her a lot and he couldn't even list why, but he did. She brought him back to life in a way. His pulse skipped when she looked into his eyes. Her smile warmed his heart. He hadn't experienced those emotions since Janet.

Though his girls made him laugh when they asked surprising questions or tried to explain something that he already knew but they thought he didn't. He couldn't stop his grin. Fatherly love puffed out his chest with pride and pleasure. The twins were his joy, but a woman's love held more than pride and pleasure, it offered contentment and the wholeness that he'd lost when Janet died.

Women had let him know they were interested and available, but the idea of spending time with another woman didn't dent his attitude. He'd loved and lost, and that experience had seemed enough to last a life time. He drew in a ragged breath. At least that's what he thought.

Yet now, Ally had aroused his interest and her presence reminded him that he was available. And still, he'd not been open with her. As his mother often reminded him, the girls need a woman in their lives and so did he. Perhaps his mom had been correct.

He straightened his back and tugged up his shoulders. Time had come to be honest with Ally. No more hiding the truth. If she balked at his admission, the situation was her loss, not... Again, he recoiled at his thoughts. Honesty plagued him as he mused what he'd just admitted. He liked Ally. More than liked her. And would miss her if she turned her back on him. But he couldn't weigh the love for his daughters against a woman he'd just met.

Today he would be honest. The girls would be back tomorrow in the late afternoon. He had little choice but to get everything out in the open. Again, shame weighted his chest and broke his heart.

Chapter 5

Ally spotted Cade pulling into her driveway a few minutes after twelve. She grabbed her purse and headed out the door, checking as he walked to his car to make sure she had her list of items she wanted to find at Grif's shop and what she needed from the grocery store in Cottonwood.

Though Cade gave a friendly nod, tension shown on his face like neon. Once she settled in, she had to ask. "Is a horse sick? I know something's wrong, Cade."

"The horses are fine. I just have a few things on my mind that I need to handle."

She shrugged. "Your shopping list must look worse than mine."

Though he flashed a faint grin, whatever bothered him remained on his face. Instead of digging deeper, she closed her mouth. She had to learn that not everyone wanted to spiel out their problems, especially if they were personal.

Cade focused on driving, his eyes glued to the road, without a flicker of acknowledgement or a word. His fingers gripped the steering wheel as if he feared it would fly off the steering rod, and his gaze never shifted anywhere near her.

She'd done something wrong, but what?

After they'd turned off Highway 179 onto Beaverhead Flat Road and continued in silence until he'd nearly reached Cornville Road, she found herself unable to hold back her concern. "Did I do something wrong, Cade? If I did, I'm sorry. I've been trying to—"

"No, Ally. No. You've done nothing wrong. I have."

Her lungs emptied, and she nearly choked. "What did I... Maybe it's not my business, Cade. I'm sorry. I keep asking questions that I have no business asking."

"Ally, please. You did nothing, and it's okay to ask." He released a puff of air and shook his head. "I did something that I can't believe, and I'm still trying to make sure I understand why. I need to tell you, but when I wrestle with how to say it, I get more confused."

"Maybe you shouldn't tell me, Cade. If it's too personal, then I don't need to know. It doesn't involve me, and—"

"But it does, Ally. It does. But that's what I'm confused about."

"You can stop giving me lessons, if that's it. I ask too much of people. I think everyone should find new experiences as exciting as I do, and as far as that goes, horseback riding isn't a new experience for you. You're an old hand at it." Panic trembled in her voice. She wanted to know what was wrong, and yet she didn't want to know.

"Let's stop for lunch somewhere and I'll be able to concentrate better. Now I need to focus on driving. This road is winding as you know, and I don't want to be distracted."

Though she longed to understand what had upset him, she couldn't demand he tell her now. "We can wait, Cade. That's fine."

Hungry? Food had vanished from her mind. The only thing she wanted is to know what troubled Cade so much that he was no longer the rancher she'd first met with the sense of humor and friendly demeanor.

She folded her hands and stared out the window, eyeing the desert landscape with homes cropping up here and there as he drove through Cornville. When the scenery changed, she stared at the rocky mountain wall that bordered the road on her side as it wound like a giant snake toward Cottonwood where they would stop to talk. Lunch for her remained questionable.

They sat in silence and the more time that passed, the more upset she became. She raked through her memory trying to imagine what she had done or said as she wandered through the hours, the days, the weeks lost in the confusing journey without a clue to where her mind should head.

The city rose in the distance and once they drove down Main Street, she spotted restaurant after restaurant, but he didn't slow down. She assumed he had a specific place in mind, and when he slowed, she spotted Grif's store. Why had he come here now when all she could think about was what he wanted to tell her?

"We're shopping now?" She failed to monitor the disbelief in her voice.

He only shrugged. "It won't take long."

She stepped from the car and followed him to the door. He held it open for her and she entered, amazed at the variety of items he sold. In one area, she spotted saddles and all the tack he would need for horse riding and training. When she turned, her gaze lit upon a line of riding pants and jeans with heavier fabric along the thigh.

Cade's focus was on the horse tack, so she moved closer. "Cade, I'll take a look at the hats and maybe some new jeans." She jutted her finger toward the area and walked away, not waiting for his response.

Disappointment raced through her as she wandered along the aisle of possible purchases. What did she need riding clothes for if her classes were ending, and she sensed that was the situation? Apparently, Cade had enough of her. Maybe another woman had asked for lessons, one who was more attractive or—

She halted her jumbled thoughts. Cade had never been a man searching for a woman while he was giving her lessons. Friendship, yes, but not dating. A dinner at her house and this trip to Cottonwood had been it. Why would she turn his image into a romancing cowboy?

The problem wasn't Cades. It was hers. What did she expect from Cade? What did she want? Her pulse tripped as it bounded through her chest. She'd found him fun, interesting, kind, and, yes, handsome. Dating had never been on her wish list. How many times did she have to remind herself that having a partner meant acting on his needs, his interests and not on her adventures and love of the unexpected.

Yet, the truth struck her. She enjoyed Cade to the point that she wanted to be with him. And yet what would happen if he didn't want to experience her fun-loving explorations. He didn't seem excited about the free hot air balloon ride he'd received from the pilot when they'd landed on his property. He cautioned her about horseback riding in the mountains. What gave him pleasure? That's what she had to know…and then face.

When she spotted Cade putting items on the cashier's counter, she forced her thoughts away from Cade and checked out a western shirt. She loved the design of flowers on the yoke and the shades of blue of the fabric. It would look great with jeans. She hurried toward the hats and studied them—Western straw hats or felt wool?

She lifted the straw hat with square blue beads along the band and placed it on her head, trying various tilts. It covered her head well, and she loved the blue beads since it matched the shirt. Whether she wore it on horseback or just to hike, it worked. Sadness weighted her chest as she sensed that her time with Cade could be coming to an end.

With the hat still on her head, she tossed the shirt over her arm and hurried to the cashier. Cade had his purchases and stood by the door. She glanced around wondering if Grif were there, but since he hadn't come out to talk with Cade, she assumed he was at his ranch. She paid for the items and grasped the bag. "Cade, I'm sorry to have taken so long. I want to—"

"Don't be sorry. I knew you wanted to look around. I came knowing exactly what I needed. You didn't. So, no apologizes necessary. I hope you didn't feel rushed seeing me standing near the door."

"No, I was finished." She had thought to purchase

the jeans, but that would have meant trying them on. Anyway, she'd lost her spirit.

He pushed open the door and she stepped outside. "There's a place right up the road where we can eat and we can walk there after we put these things in the car."

She only nodded, surprised that he seemed less tense than he had earlier.

"By the way, I like your hat." He grinned. "It's great for riding and for walking in the hot sun."

Again, she nodded and dropped her package in the trunk as he had done.

"I thought we could go to Hog Wild Barbeque. They have everything - salads, burgers, sandwiches and not everything is barbequed. Does that sound good?"

"Sure, that's fine. I love salads and interesting sandwiches."

He motioned ahead, and they continued in silence that unsettled her stomach. Tension built until she wanted to scream. But before she said something she would regret, he stopped and turned to the doorway. In the window, she saw the sign, Hog Wild BBQ.

♥

Cade held the door open as Ally stepped into the air conditioning. The temperature had heightened as afternoon arrived, and he already felt in a sweat dealing with the issues that burdened his mind. He would have to be stupid to not recognize the tension that had struck Ally, and he knew it was his fault. He longed to explain and yet he still couldn't understand his hesitation to get it out in the open.

The cashier pointed to a free table along a side wall away from the windows, and he was grateful. Heat permeated the windows, and they didn't need that. He was already in enough heat with Ally for ruining the day. A waiter stopped and handed them a menu, then took their drink orders. When he left, they perused the menu in silence.

After a few moments, Ally set her menu down. "I'm not really hungry."

His heart sank. He knew why. He'd upset her with his tense actions and his confused expression. "It's my fault, Ally. Please have something. Anything. If you don't, I'll feel rotten, although I deserve it."

"No, it's just me."

"Ally, I've acted like a jerk. I've not talked about people who are important to me, and now you've become important to me and I—"

"I what?" Her expression twisted into confusion—wrinkled brow, squinted eyes, downturned mouth. She wasn't the attractive woman he'd come to know.

"We've become friends. I like you. Like you a lot, and I've made you feel badly. You've added some new interest in my life. Not only did you want to learn to ride, but you want to learn about horses. I love horses and to find a woman who has the same interest is something new for me. You're special."

"Me? I don't see it, but thank you."

Before he could respond, the waiter returned with their drinks and took the food orders. When he left, Cade took a moment to get his thoughts in order.

"Ally, let's start today over again. My problem is I have two other females in my life that I've never mentioned."

"You're married?" Her eyebrows raised to her hairline.

"No. Not that. I was married. I told you that. Janet

died, but we had two daughters. Twins. They're seven years old."

Ally's expression skewed even more. "You mean you have two girls. Where are they? I've never seen one of them since we got to know each other."

"They were visiting their Grandma in Phoenix. They love it there in the summer since the Village tends to be retired couples with adult children. The girls have friends in Phoenix and enjoy all kinds of fun things. Plus, my mom loves to have them visit."

"Oh." Her frown changed to another negative expression, but he couldn't name the emotion.

"You'll meet them today perhaps. They'll be home in the late afternoon."

She pressed her lips together and shook her head. "I see. So, the riding lessons will not continue, I assume. You'll have too much responsibility."

"No, that's not the case." He studied her face with a heavy heart. Her attitude disappointed him, but didn't surprise him. He'd feared this would happen, and that's why he'd been unable to tell her. He understood that even better now.

"But how can you—"

"I have a sitter come in when I need to, and when school starts, they're at school all day so I have free time then."

"I see."

His eyes searched hers, and instead of swallowing all the questions that hung in his mind, he opened his mouth. "You don't like children."

"Why do you say that?"

His eyes shot open, reminding him of biscuits from a tube. "Why wouldn't I? If you liked kids, you might say you couldn't wait to meet them, or kids that age were interesting or something."

"I've never really been around kids that much, Cade. I don't have any children in my life so it's uncharted territory."

"Then it's an adventure, Ally. You love adventure."

"Kids are adventure?" Her eyes widened. "Well, that's new to me. But then what do I know?"

"Once you get to know them, you'll see what I mean."

"Are you sure you want the children to know me? I'm inexperienced to the core, and I've never yearned for the experience."

He looked away trying to sort his thoughts. "But it is a new experience, just as I said. Maybe it will be fun. You know, a challenge."

He sensed she'd tried to turn a sneer into a grin, but she'd failed. As he studied her, reality settled in his mind. Why did he want to hang on to the friendship? If Ally made it difficult for his girls, it would be very difficult for him. He should just step back and allow the new relationship to fade away.

His chest grew heavy. But did he want to?

"Cade, ignore my foolish comments and questions if you can. You surprised me with your admission today, and I keep asking myself why you would hide that important fact about yourself." She lowered her head, then inched it upward. "I suppose you had your reason."

"That's why I had trouble all day, Ally. I was ashamed of myself for not talking about the girls. A good father would want to brag about his children or at least mention them. I didn't do that, and I've had to ask myself why, also."

"Did you find an answer?"

"I suppose I already told you. When we met you let me know that you were a person who loved your freedom. You enjoy adventures and excitement…even danger. I found that interesting since I've had wonderful experiences with the horses and learning about them. You know how much goes into training them and riding them. But I don't see that as adventure."

"It has been for me. The horses were something new."

The waiter appeared with their selections, and Cade was grateful that Ally had ordered a salad. He offered to come back and refill their drinks, but they said there was no need at the same time. He smiled and went on his way.

"And you were also, Cade."

"I was what?"

"New to me also."

She grinned, and he loved seeing her face brighten.

He grinned back, muttering a thank you, but his mind was filled with their previous topic. "I'm glad you find riding an adventure, Ally, but think it through. Yes, horses are very interesting and there is a lot to learn and skill to be a good rider. But that has nothing to do with freedom. When you own horses and board other people's horses, you don't have total freedom unless you can get someone qualified to care for them while you're heading for a new adventure. On top of that you add two seven-year-old girls, and life changes. Do you understand?"

"Sort of, I guess." Her frown returned, and she

lowered her eyes to the salad and picked up her fork.

"Remember what I said earlier. When I met you, I found you interesting and I grew to enjoy your company and liked you very much. You added a spark to my life, but Ally that spark will be gone later today since the girls are back. I have to give them time too, and I can't join you in a new experience at the sound of 'Getty-up.'"

A faint grin lifted the edge of her lips. "I don't think you'll hear a Getty-up from me, but I do see what you mean."

He stared at the burger he'd ordered and sadly, he wasn't hungry either, but he took a bite and forced it down followed by a drink of water.

He watched Ally shift the vegetables and some diced chicken around on her plate, and she finally took a bite also. The eating plans had been bad timing.

After another bite which went down easier, he sorted his thoughts. "Ally, I know we have more to say, but let me finish with this. I'm a dad first and then a man who enjoys horses and, to be honest, your company. But I don't know how you'll feel about everything once the girls arrive. I'm anxious to see the twins, but I'm not anxious to have you wave and walk away forever."

"Cade, don't say that. You know we've had lots of fun and—"

"That's the point. We have, but our fun will be different now. I can't put my girls in a locked room so I can go out and have fun. It means babysitters and not much on the spur of the moment. "Miss Allysa Grant, you are a spur of the moment woman."

Again, her head lowered, and a lengthy breath

dragged from her lungs. "I am, but do I have to be every minute of the day?" She appeared to be asking herself the question. "No. I work a job, and it needs me to be on top of things. I can't have adventures at a patient's expense. I've been able to work a variety of hours, so I suppose it seems as if I don't have a job, but I do."

"I didn't mean to belittle your work. Anyone in the medical field approaches it seriously. It's part of the life and death work you do."

Her gaze sought his and she didn't blink. "Let's be open here. Would you like me to stay away then? I would miss the horses, but maybe I can visit Grif's ranch or—"

"That's something you must decide, Ally." She would miss the horses? What about him? And Grif? "That's not what I want to have happen. I'd love you to get to know my twins. I hope that you find them fun and maybe a bit adventurous too."

"Thanks. And Cade, I care about you, too. It's not just horses and riding. It's our friendship. You've added some excitement in my life, but knowing you and spending time with you has made you more important. You're a part of my life, but the time has been short. So, I don't want to be rash either. I need to give you time with your girls, but I hope that I can meet them, and we can see what happens."

His pulse jogged, hearing her sound more positive than she had. "I'm for that, Ally." But as he reviewed what she had said, maybe her comment was that positive. What happens could be good or bad. It could be hello or goodbye. Why hadn't he suggested they could work at it, and not just see what happens?

♥

When Cade dropped her off at home, Ally grabbed her leftover box, waved and watched him drive away. What she'd expected to be a day that she would remember with a smile had turned into a day she didn't want to remember.

She slipped the salad into the refrigerator, poured a glass of water, and sank into a living room chair, her mind reeling with how her life had changed in a moment.

Her shock, hearing Cade had seven-year-old twin girls, knocked her off her feet. He'd given no inkling that he had kids. Not one word. Not one comment that she'd pondered as to what he meant. Or had he?

She tried to go back in time and think about their conversations. Most of them were about horses, riding and silly, playful comments that she'd enjoyed.

Now what she'd anticipated as a new hill in her life had flattened into a dry pasture. She would miss her time with Cade and the riding lessons, and now she'd purchased a Western shirt and straw hat... What had she done? Tension knotted her memory, but then she snapped her fingers. She'd forgotten her packages.

She pulled herself up from the chair and stood a moment. With the girls coming later today, she needed to get over there and pick up her purchases. She motivated her feet to the front door and looked outside, hoping Cade had spotted the package and would bring it back. She leaned out of the door and saw nothing on the road. He probably forgot as she did.

Without anymore questions, she grasped the knob and stepped outside. The bright sun struck her arms, but a breeze whisked away any serious heat. She stepped onto the road and headed up the hill to the ranch. She loved the view of Lee Mountain, and again her dream returned of riding Bliss or another horse up the road and onto the mountain, but the reality washed it away. She'd never ride well enough without more lessons.

If Cade refused the lessons, she could ask Grif. But did she want to? He was a nice man, in fact, she'd thought about somehow finagling an introduction of Grif to Marcy. She never dated, and yet she seemed much more a type of woman who could be a good wife and mother. She kept her feet on the ground.

Her gaze drifted from the mountain to the meadow stretching in front of her, and Cade's ranch came into view. She paused as she reached his gate, questioning her wisdom to interfere with him welcoming his daughters if they arrived before she left. She shrugged. Not likely and then what difference was there. She'd be gone in a moment.

She opened the gate, closed it and strode up the driveway. She looked toward the stable but didn't see anyone or any action so she assumed Cade was inside. As she approached the door, it flew open, and she stopped cold. Two cute faces grinned at her from behind the screen. Caught off guard, she stood a moment unable to speak.

"Hello. Is your daddy home?"

Before they responded, Cade scooted them out of the way and gazed at her as if assessing her attitude. "I found your package."

"Sorry to have rushed over, I realized I'd forgotten it and didn't know if—"

"I'm glad you came. I was going to run it over later, but since you're here, please come in. You can meet my girls and my mom."

His mom, too. "Goodness, I didn't notice her car."

"It's back there, and as I said, I'm glad you came."

She managed a pleasant look, though wishing she'd not charged over so fast...or at least called first. She would have been prepared.

Cade beckoned her inside, and she did as he asked totally unprepared to face his company...his family. The girls stood nearby looking her over as if she were a new puppy. That aroused her curiosity and seated in a chair was a sweet looking white-haired woman with a lovely smile.

Ally managed to smile back and prayed her look was sincere. The woman's contagious smile drew her in. "Hello." She moved toward his mother. "I'm Allysa Grant. Ally to my friends." She extended her hand, and his mother grasped it with a warm grip.

"What a lovely surprise. As you know I'm Cade's mom, grandmother to the girls, and I'm Eva." She chuckled. "You can't shorten that."

"No, you can't." Eva motioned for her to be seated, and she settled in the nearest chair as she switched her focus to the two inquisitive girls. "And I know that one of you is Jolie and the other Chloe. Is that right?"

"I'm Chloe and I'm the oldest." She grinned, her bowed lips forming a curve and her light bluish green eyes sparkling.

"Oldest by one minute, Daddy said." She frowned at Chloe. "I'm Jolie."

Though they had very similar features, they weren't identical though both their dark brown hair had streaks of golden wheat-tones running through it.

"I've heard about you from your dad, and it's nice

to meet you in person…and your grandma. I hear you like to visit her."

"We don't have a lot of friends here." Jolie shrugged. "Daddy says most people are old."

Ally couldn't halt an unexpected laugh that slipped from her. "Lots of people are, but I think I'm still in the middle…sort of like your daddy."

Chloe bustled closer to her. "You don't look old either. Can you have babies?"

Her head flew back as her eyes sought Cade's.

"Chloe." Cade moved closer and captured her gaze. "I don't think that's a question you want to ask people when you first meet them."

"Why? Can't she have babies."

Ally came to Cade's rescue. "I suppose I could, Chloe, but I'm not married so I'll have to think about that if the time comes."

Chloe appeared to mull over her response. "Then maybe you could if you were married."

Jolie muscled her way between Chloe and her. "Daddy just said not to ask personal questions, Chloe, and you're supposed to be the oldest."

The look Jolie gave her sister caused a chuckle from everyone but Chloe.

Cade stepped in and turned the two to face him. "Girls, why don't you go and unpack. Put your dirty clothes in the hamper and—"

"Grandma washed our clothes before we packed to come home." Jolie grinned at her grandma.

"You did, Mom?"

"Didn't want to send home a bag of laundry. Anyway, the girls helped. They tossed them in the washer and into the dryer when they were ready, and they folded them. I only turned on the machines and put in the soap."

Cade's gaze swept across everyone. "Then thanks to all of you."

"Except Ally. She didn't do anything."

Cade rolled his eyes. "Thank you, Chloe for your correction."

Ally pressed her lips together not to let out a muffled guffaw. These girls were as precocious as they came. Yet, surprisingly, she did find them interesting. "Well, I'm sure you all have things to do, so I should collect my package and get back home."

"Can't you stay?" Chloe shifted closer and rested her hands on the chair arm. "We could play a game."

"I'm sure your dad has work to do, and I'm guessing your grandma would like to visit with your daddy too."

"Grandma and Daddy can talk, and we could play Old Maid. Do you know how to play it?"

By then Chloe had nuzzled up beside her too. Though they gave her a chuckle, she tried to imagine living with these two day in and day out. Her grin might turn to pulling out her hair.

"I played Old Maid when I was younger, but—"

"Girls." Cade's voice had turned into a father's voice, sterner than she'd ever heard him speak. "How about unpacking and give Ally a few minutes to talk with Grandma and with me. Okay?"

Two pairs of shoulders drooped as frowns settled on their bowed lips. They ambled across the room to a hallway, looking as downtrodden as Jack Sparrow walking the plank. Cade watched them go into the room and he headed that way too.

Ally looked up and saw his mother gazing at her with a curious grin. "Do the girls wear you out?"

"If I let them. They do have friends there so they're outside much of the day or going somewhere with the friends. They're good about asking if they can go, and I know the parents so it's always nice for a little quiet."

Ally grinned this time. "Yes, quiet must be rare with two active young ladies."

"It is, but when they come home, it's mighty lonely until I get used to it again."

Ally understood that. "I live alone too, so I understand."

Eva's grin faded. "Are you a widow or—"

"I've never married. I've led a busy life with work and always seeking something new to explore. Cade says I'm a spur-of-the-moment woman. I know I couldn't do that if I had children."

"No but there are other rewards, but then I'm sure you know that."

She wasn't as sure, but she let it drop. "It's nice that you have such a good relationship with the girls. I find that a wonderful gift to them and to Cade."

"Yes, we do, and speaking of relationships, I'm surprised Cade's never told me about you. I didn't realize—"

"There's not much to tell, really. I live down the road a ways, and Cade's been giving me riding lessons. I've become very fond of the horses."

"Riding lessons?" Eva tilted her head as if she were trying to find a place to file that information. "You seem friendlier than teacher and student."

"Well, I suppose we do enjoy each other's company. We went shopping in Cottonwood together at another rancher's store. That's why I came over today. I left my packages in his car."

"Shopping? That sounds like an odd way to spend time together. No dinners or—"

"Ah, yes. I had Cade over for dinner one evening. That's all he wanted as payment for my horseback riding lessons."

"And it was a good dinner, Mom." Cade came through the doorway, an odd look on his face as if he wished he had been in the room earlier.

"I was telling, Ally, here, that you never mentioned having dinner with her or...going shopping."

Eva's expression was almost laughable.

"Mom, it's hard to make a romance out of that, isn't it?" He turned to Ally and shook his head. "My mom thinks the girls need a mother and I need a wife, so duck, Ally. She might pounce."

"Cade." His mother shook her finger at him as she probably did when he was seven. "I don't pounce. I'm just thinking of what's best for my granddaughters and their father. Although he has other ideas."

"Mom, I have no ideas, actually, and I was only teasing you. I know you love us and want us to have good lives."

Ally glanced away wishing she could make an escape. She had no idea whether being there stirred up this particular discussion or if the topic was Eva's typical conversation. Whichever it was, the subject made her horribly uncomfortable.

She shifted in the chair and leaned forward. "Listen, you have some serious talking to do, and I really need to go. I just dropped by for my—"

"No. No, Dear." Eva flailed her hands. "Please

don't leave. I'd like to get to know you better. You seem like a lovely woman, and you were so patient with the girls."

Patient? She had little choice. "The twins are very cute and eager as children are. How can a person not be patient with their inquisitiveness?" She could easily but she'd been cornered.

"That's so kind of you." She shifted her focus to Cade. "You see, Son, this is the kind of person that you need to find." A grin stole to her face. "Well, I guess you already have."

"Mother, could we cut this topic. I'm sure Ally does not want to sit here and listen to our family discussion, and anyway, she said she needed to go." He eyed Ally with another eye roll.

Ally found the courage to stand and approach his mother. "Eva, it was so nice meeting you, but I do need to return home since I have tons to do. Perhaps we can chat another time."

"Dear, I hope I haven't made you uncomfortable."

Her pulse jumped a foot. "Goodness no, as I said, I only stopped by for the package." She'd lied, a great big fat lie, but she had little choice. Poor Eva wanted to run Cade's life, and he didn't seem like a man who would let her do that.

Cade stepped in and took her arm. "Follow me. I set you shopping bag near the door so I would remember to drop it off. "

Cade handed her the package and opened the door. As she stepped out, he followed her. "Ally, I'm so sorry. My mother will not let that topic die. She's determined that I find a wife and a mother for my girls. I'm so sorry. She put you on the spot, and I don't like that at all, but she's my mom and—"

"Cade, don't worry. I understand. Your mother is a strong-willed lady, and she adores you and the twins. I can understand why. I couldn't help but smile at the girls' curiosity and blunt questions. I had to hold back from laughing."

"Laughing? Are you sure? I wondered if you were going to let out a scream."

She pressed her lips together, and then gave up and responded. "To be honest, I'd thought of that, but I was able to contain myself."

"Well, I'm proud of you. I owe you." He slipped his arm around her shoulder and gave her a hug.

New sensations rolled down her limbs and dropped to the pit of her stomach. An earthy scent washed over her as he held her close. Aftershave? Men's soap? Her senses tingled as if she'd been sitting in a field of flowers with the scent of heat, soil, and the floral fragrance.

"Please apologize for my leaving so abruptly, Cade. I do like your mother, and I enjoyed meeting the girls. I can see you have your hands full, and I understand now why your life is not spur of the moment."

"You got that right." He gave her another squeeze as his eyes captured hers.

The muscles of her legs quivered and became as unsteady as a melting candle. She feared he noticed her unsteadiness. "They're very cute, Cade. I can see they have some likeness to you."

"I'm not sure if that's good or bad." He grinned.

"It's good. They have your dark brown hair, the greenish color of your eyes...although theirs is mixed with blue, and they have your wonderful smile."

"Wonderful, huh?"

"Okay, you have a nice smile."

He rested his hand on her shoulder. "So now I'm being demoted."

"It's hard to make you happy, Mr. Murphy, but then I sense it's some of your Irish blarney."

"Ah-ha. You've already caught on." He eased back as his expression became more serious. "I have to admit, Ally, that my mother is right. You would make a wonderful wife, but I know you've avoided that commitment, and I understand. If I find a woman someday that I'm attracted to, she'll have to be as patient and fun loving as you are to survive my girls and my sense of humor."

She opened her mouth to speak, but the words stuck in her throat. She was far from patient, although she had to admit today she'd done a pretty good job. Fun-loving was more accurate. But that wasn't what befuddled her. His reference that she would make a wonderful wife caught her totally off-guard.

Needing to respond, she dug deep. "You are very kind, and you lie very sincerely."

He clasped her cheeks between his palms and leaned so close his eyes met hers with only a fraction to spare. "I never lie. You can't accept the truth. Think about it, Ally, and also, don't think because my girls are here that I don't plan to give you lessons. We'll work something out. I promise."

Her lungs drained of air. He'd said so much more than she ever expected to hear from him, and now he offered to continue her lessons. "Cade, thank you. Please don't think that my lessons are your responsibility. It started as one of my fun activities, and in the process, I grew to love your horses. That surprised me. I've loved the time we've spent with them, and even shopping with you was nice."

"It was. I'm glad you've enjoyed learning the techniques of riding and about horses. That's now something we have in common. I would miss not having you in my life, Ally. Just remember that." He put his hand on the door knob and eased it open. "I'll see you soon. Okay?"

"Okay, and I'll look forward to it." She stepped through the doorway but then stopped. "I almost forgot. Tell the girls I'll take an Old Maid rain check.

He stood a moment, his gaze capturing hers until she wanted to throw her arms around his neck, but she had to remember her goals and her lifestyle. Cade had two seven-year-old girls. What did she have to offer them? Nothing."

Chapter 6

"Daddy, let's do something fun." Chloe hung on to the edge of his recliner, her lip stuck out like a water pitcher.

"Get creative, Chloe. You have games to play. You can go outside as long as you stay close to the ranch and you can visit the horses. I'll give you carrots to feed them. How's that?"

"Okay, but that's not what I mean."

Jolie wiggled her way into the conversation. "We want to play with kids, Daddy, and there aren't any. Let's move to Phoenix where Grandma lives and—"

"Girls, this is your life. I'm not moving. I have a business here and that's that. When school starts you'll be back with your school friends, and why didn't you make plans with some of them before summer vacation starts. They have to live somewhere in the area. Let's give that some thought."

Chloe jerked her arms from the chair. "Now you tell us. Can't you find out things, Daddy? We didn't think about summer. I know some live in Sedona where all the stores are."

"That's a lot of homes, Sweety. Let me think about this okay, and while I do, how about feeding some carrots to the horses."

Jolie released a long breath, her face as hangdog as Chloe's. "Fine. But that won't take long."

"Dear Lord, I know it won't."

"Can that lady come over and—"

"Her name's Ally, Chloe. Can't you remember anything?"

"Okay, it's Ally. Let's have her come over and play with—"

"Girls, Ally works at a hospital, and she has a house to keep up and adult things to do."

"Boring." Both girls whined out the word at the same time.

"Right, adult life is sometimes boring." He touched each girls' cheek and turned them to face him. "I asked if you would give me a few minutes to think. Carrot time, and maybe I'll think of something."

"Okay." Jolie did a quick turn and headed for the kitchen.

He joined the girls and handed out the carrots. When they left, he had a few minutes to think. He stepped into the laundry room and pulled out a few newspapers from the past couple of days. Somewhere churches were having Day Camp for kids and some called in Vacation Bible School. He needed someplace he could trust.

He carried the papers to the kitchen table and scanned them, looking for the ads he'd seen. Finally, he spotted two that weren't too far away, Methodist and Lutheran churches. His heavy spirit eased, and he drew in a lengthy breath, grateful that this could work.

He pulled out his cell phone and gave the first one a call. He wanted to cheer when he heard the welcoming tone of the woman's voice and jotted down what he had to do to sign them up. The ride was short, and he could drop them off and pick them up later in the day. That would give him time to handle the horses and to give Ally her riding lessons.

With the reprieve and his phone in hand, he hit Ally's number. It rang five times before voice mail kicked in and he remembered she would be at work. Still, he left the message that soon the lessons would be back so try to schedule the time. With that done, he leaned back and waited for the bang of the door and his twins pouting again with nothing to do.

♥

Ally sat in the hospital cafeteria nibbling on the lunch she'd created from the salad bar. That had been one thing she enjoyed, and it was good for her. For someone who loved adventure, food hadn't been one of them. She stuck to healthy choices usually. Sitting alone for once, she drew out her phone and spotted a voice mail. When she hit on it, Cade's message spurted out and she hurried to lower the volume. Two people nearby had given her one of those looks.

Her pulse skipped as he told her that he was working on a plan to entertain the girls and be able to give her the lessons. She enjoyed being with the horses, but she loved even more being with Cade. That reality aroused her concern, and yet she did little to change it. All she had to do is keep her emotions intact and just have a good time with a pleasant man.

"Hi, when did you get here?" Marcy slipped into the chair across from her.

"I traded lunches with one of the other nurses. I should have told you. Sorry."

"That's okay." Marcy lifted her fork and held it above her food. "What's wrong? You look as if you've lost your best friend."

A puff of air escaped her lungs before she could form words. "Nothing except my confused mind and crazy imagination."

"Cade, right?" Marcy's eyes brightened as a faint grin curved her lips.

"No…well, yes, but it's nothing."

"Oh, yes it is. You don't look that upset about nothing."

"Come on, Marcy. You know I've spent a lot of time with Cade and it's been fun. But I'm facing the truth, and it's putting my head in a vice. I can't think straight."

"I think that's called falling in love."

She drew back and held up her hand. "Stop." Looking in Marcy's eyes, she had to admit that Marcy had touched on the truth. "Look, as I said, I'm confused and I'm sorry to be so sharp with you. You know I'm a woman of the moment, anything for fun and excitement, but suddenly my life changed when I met Cade. I enjoy the horses but even more, I really enjoy his company. My crazy mind has headed in directions I don't want to go."

"That's what love does, Ally. If not love, real attraction. The guy is a nice man. You've told me his attributes a few times, He's kind, thoughtful, funny and good looking. Even that description is telling."

"But the scenario has changed. He has the girls, seven-year-old twins, and that means his life isn't really free. He has heavy duty responsibility and—"

"And he has to be a dad as well as a horse trainer

and a man falling in love."

"Marcy, I don't know about falling in love. Cade has been great, and we have fun together, but life isn't all fun, I realize that and especially when a person has kids."

"What makes you think that having children can't be fun? Kids are amazing. They are funny and inquisitive. They keep adults on their toes and forces them to learn the answers to their kids' questions. Kids enjoy new experiences. Sure, there are times when they get cranky or whiny but that's not most of the time. You need to read up on what having a child means."

"I met the girls, by the way."

"You did? Wow. What happened?" Marcy leaned closer, her lunch still sitting below the extended fork.

"They were inquisitive as you said, and they did make me laugh, but they are time-consuming and jumping into something without a lot of plans won't work."

"Is that the most important thing in life? Isn't being with the man you love the ultimate pleasure of a commitment?"

Why try to fool Marcy? "Okay, honesty. I wanted to be with him, and yet I'm certain that my life of acting on the moment and trying crazy and even dangerous things would come to an end if I tied myself up with a man who has two seven-year-old twin girls.

Her mind reeled as she held her breath. "Marcy, and the hardest thing to face is Cade has never given me any inkling that he had any intention of a relationship more than friendship. Never."

"Has he kissed you?"

"No, the closest he got was putting his arm around

my shoulder and later giving me a hug."

Marcy's jaw sagged. "Oh, I thought with all the time together something might have happened."

"He enjoys my company, he says, and also, he'd miss having me in his life." She shrugged. "That's about it."

"That sounds positive to me, Ally. Give it time. The man lost his wife and was left with those two little girls. He's raised them on his own, and they have been his focus. It's hard to recognize that life is more than that. Being with you, he's noticed how nice it is to be with an adult woman, and he's admitted two important things—enjoying your company and missing you if you weren't in his life. Wow, that says a lot."

"You really think so?"

Marcy nodded and finally dug her fork in the helping of pasta on her plate.

"I just got a voice mail from him, and it was good news."

Her fork lowered again as Marcy's eyes widened. "Well, tell me."

"Cade said he's working on a plan that will entertain the girls part of the day, and he can give me more riding lessons."

"I'd hoped to hear a bit more than that, but yes, that's good since it means he knows he has to keep his girls busy for you two to have quality time together."

Ally's spirit lifted. Marcy was right. "Let's see how that goes." A smile tugged at her usual tight lips and she relaxed and let the smile come. "That does make me happy."

"It should." Marcy took another bite and when she swallowed, she lifted her head. "What surprises me is your change of heart. Marriage has always been out of the question for you and now I'm hearing a new story plus this one involves children."

The comment smacked Ally in the head. Marcy was right. She'd spent her life determined to be the fun-loving person she has always been. How could she drop that plan so easily?

"Maybe I'll come to my senses." Ally turned her focus to the last of her salad without saying more.

Though Marcy remained quiet a moment, obviously she wanted to say something, but she didn't. She delved into her lunch and let the topic die.

That was for best.

♥

Cade headed into the church with the girls, who weren't totally thrilled but they were willing to give it a try. He had to stand in a line near the door waiting to register them, and then couldn't believe when he reached the front, the fact that he had twins seemed to be of interest to the woman who registered them. Apparently, his daughters were the only twins, and the woman seemed disappointed that they weren't identical. He, on the other hand, thanked the Lord. Keeping track of the two was confusing enough without one pretending to be the other and he feared they might have tried that.

"Can the girls stay today, then?" Cade watched the woman make name tags for his daughters. The woman nodded. "Goodness, yes. The summer program began yesterday but they didn't miss much, and I'm sure they'll have a wonderful time. We do all kinds of things here from games to new experiences, readings and more."

"Wonderful. The summer is a long time, and we live on a ranch, so we don't have close neighbors with children."

"They will find new friends here." She handed each girl a name tag with a sticky back that she exposed. "Tomorrow they'll have a pin on name tag." She gave the girls a pleasant smile while he helped them stick the tag on their tops. He hoped the tags would stay in place. He often found that kind of tag stuck to the bottom of his shoe.

Though the girls had been eager, their expressions now indicated they were dubious about being left there alone without him at their sides. "Girls, have fun and I'll be back at four to take you home. Enjoy the day, and I'm sure you'll find lots of fun things to do."

Without waiting for their questions or decisions to not stay, he leaned over, gave each one a hug, then turned his back and darted for the door.

Once in the car, he prayed they would enjoy themselves so tomorrow wouldn't present two girls crying that they didn't want to go back. He gazed at the church entrance pleased that the twins hadn't chased after him.

Silly how protective he felt at times, but he wanted them to have fun…just as he wanted to have fun time too. As soon as the idea of fun struck his mind, his thoughts shifted to Ally. Though tempted to call her, he decided to send a text instead. If she were at work, the text would be there for her to read.

He hit the message button and poked each letter with one finger to let her know that tomorrow he would be able to give her a riding lesson in the late morning if she had the day off, and if she had today off, he asked her to call him. He sent the message, and then started the car and pulled away.

Ally filled his mind while questions billowed. He wished he had the answers, but only time could offer a hint of what was to be. She'd done well with the girls, and they liked her. He grinned as he recalled them wanting her to come over to play. He'd have to tell her that.

When he arrived home, he headed for the stable to take care of the horses. The stable duties were a daily job and one that he often enjoyed despite the awful work of mucking out the stalls. As he shoveled, he heard a ting and paused to eye his phone. A text message from Ally caused a riffle through his chest to his gut, a sensation he never understood.

He leaned the shovel against the stall and hit the message icon to read what she'd written. He read that she was on a strange schedule and would be home around noon today. He texted her to call him when she arrived or just drop by. Thinking of the past, he recalled that high school and dating hadn't been as exciting as he experienced now as a man. Even if seeing Ally wasn't a date, she'd become a diversion that took him from his previously scheduled life to one with more variety. So different from his routine life before he'd met her.

The girls certainly keep him hopping, but Ally's presence had no similarity to his girls. They were a given. He adored them and took care of them, and what they did either made him proud or angry. With Ally, he was neither proud nor angry. Her presence stimulated him, and he sought a new kind of contentment. Whether a normal reaction or abnormal, he might never know since who would he ask?

He wished he understood his feelings for Ally. She'd been very clear that commitment to a relationship would never darken her door. He'd met her only a couple months ago, and yet his life changed. He wasn't the man he'd been, willing to settle back and raise his girls while working the ranch.

His girls would always be part of his life, and he enjoyed the ranch, but adding a new vista to his daily existence—crawling out of the box, traveling, grasping new experiences—as Ally would call it, having an adventure—now stayed on the edge of his thoughts. Could he be a man who enjoyed unexpected experiences?

The day Ally arrived in the hot air balloon, he'd been gifted with two free balloon rides. He would never have considered such a thing, but having the tickets meant using them, giving them away, or wasting them.

The ride wasn't for children. If he used the tickets himself, he would have to find someone to go with him, and who would be better than Ally, a woman who sought excitement. Maybe one day, but not now. His girls were enough excitement.

He grasped the shovel again and returned to work, knowing that noon wasn't that far off. He finished the last stall, tossed in fresh hay for each horse and gave each a little attention and later he would put them in the coral for some exercise. No riding today unless that's what Ally wanted to do. Today, he would rather sit and talk.

Inside he grabbed a slab of lunchmeat, slapped it on a piece of bread with a little butter, and took a bite. Anticipating Ally's visit had changed his appetite. Food was a side dish while Ally was the main course. He closed his eyes, trying to dig deep into his senses and sort out what was going on. He barely knew her, and yet they'd bonded in a way he didn't understand.

Getting married again or even getting involved again had fallen into the deep recesses of his mind. Janet had been a wonderful wife, taken too soon, and his grief had been a nightmare, something he hid in the dark. He had to be the light for his three-year-old girls, girls who'd lost their mother and didn't understand, but then neither did he.

Time had passed while his pain tended to ebb, but it was not forgotten. Being so young, the girls somehow adjusted to spending time with their Grandma or sitters he'd found—women—willing to take on the job for pay. He would always be grateful.

Now their lives had fallen into a pattern, running smoothly through the hours, days and weeks, and yet meeting Ally had put a bump in his road. A big bump with too many unanswered questions and too much he didn't understand.

He swallowed the last of his pitiful sandwich when he heard a rap on the door. His heart lurched as he approached and with no surprise saw Ally standing there wearing her new Western shirt. "Hi, come in." He pushed the door wider and she came in with a grin."I didn't hear you drive up."

"I didn't. I walked it's less than a mile." She stepped inside and then did a few circle turns. "What do you think? Will I pass for a Cowgirl?"

He couldn't help but smile at her pose. "Well, howdy pardner. You're lookin' mighty fine."

"Thank ya'll." She faced him. "I didn't bring my

new hat. I feared it was too late and too hot to ride so I didn't think I'd need it. I just wanted you to see the shirt and get your approval."

"You have my approval, Ma'am."

She gave him a playful punch along with a chuckle. "You're in a good mood."

"Guess I am. I found a summer vacation program for the girls at a church nearby and I signed them up. So far so good. No phone calls."

"That's a great idea. They'll meet some kids too, as well as have fun."

"That's my hope. And by the way, I don't want to forget. This plan was motivated by their whining that they were bored, and I didn't have fun things for them to do. So, guess what their idea was."

She gave him a blank look. "I have no idea. Buy them a dog?"

"Whoa, don't mention that or I'll be at the dog shelter bringing home a Great Dane. They'll want a big one that looks like a small horse."

"They would love a dog. Why not surprise them?"

"Okay, you can get a dog, and the girls can—"

Ally flexed her hand like a police officer. "No one said I wanted a dog. We're talking about you."

"Maybe, we shouldn't. Let's talk about you." He pointed to the living room sofa. "Have a seat?"

She faltered a moment, and then sank into an easy chair. "This conversation began because you were going to tell me the girls' idea of what they wanted to do."

He palmed the top of his head, amazed that he'd drifted so far from the topic. "Right. They wanted me to ask you to come over and play with them."

Her eyes widened as her mouth curved to a grin. "You're kidding me."

"Not one bit. I had to explain that you were an adult who worked and didn't have time to play games."

She covered her face with her hands, chuckling and then peeked between her fingers. "Those poor girls. They must really be bored to want to play with me. If they only knew…" She dropped her hands with a look he didn't understand.

"What?"

Her frown deepened. "I'm not sure what you're asking."

"You said if they only knew. My question is only knew what?"

"Oh." She lowered her eyes again before inching her head upward. "I'm a grouch, I suppose. I don't play games and I'm not really good with kids either."

"Who told you that?" He studied her expression as she thought.

"No one, I guess. I just know that I'm at a loss when it comes to children."

"Everyone is until they have the experience and get to know the kids. Then a person can change."

"If the person wants to change."

He drew back, this time a frown growing on his face. "Why wouldn't a person…or let's say you…why wouldn't you want to change?"

Ally pressed her lips together a moment as if trying to come up with a response that she couldn't seem to find. "That's sort of dumb, isn't it?"

He nodded. "You made a good impression on Chloe and Jolie, or they wouldn't have asked me to invite you over to play games with them. So yes, it's dumb."

The look on her face melted to a grin. "Well, la-de-dah."

That made him laugh. "Okay, not changing the subject, but I am changing the subject."

"Talk about dumb."

He arched his brow and managed to hold back a smile. "We don't have a lot of time, but do you want to try and ride today or is tomorrow better? That is if the girls want to go back to the church."

"I think they will, and yes tomorrow would be good, but I'd love to go out and visit the horses. Can we do that?"

He jumped up, glad she'd asked. "Yes, and I almost forgot I want to put them in the corral so they get a little exercise. With that shirt on, you can help."

"Is the shirt a requirement?"

"No, but you look good in it. The horses will know you're a real cowgirl."

She waved her hand as if swiping away his comment and rose. "Let's go."

He stepped closer and linked his arm with hers as stepped outside into the pleasant sunshine and ambled to the stable. For the first time in years, the sense of having a partner, a companion, a lovely woman on his arm warmed his heart.

And he almost believed that Ally liked the girls better than she wanted to admit.

♥

Watching the horses run free in the corral gave Ally a sense of freedom too. In her lifetime, horses had never been an interest of hers, and yet in the short time she'd enjoyed the riding lessons, she'd learned so much from the horses. They were like people with their own personalities and their own way of expressing themselves and responding to her method of communication. She could tighten her knee and Bliss knew she wanted her to go fast. She could lean back, and the horse knew she wanted her to slow down.

The process had been amazing, and her awareness of the horses' beauty had touched her. If she had time and space, she would love to own a horse. In fact, she'd given it thought since she'd been away from her lessons. She missed being around the hard-working animals who, in their own way, showed love to the humans.

Maybe she'd become overzealous as usual. A new experience tended to heighten her life. Why had she spent her days searching for adventures? The event happens and then it's gone. No more an adventure. It's become a reality. Could it be that her desire for excitement and adventure had been fulfilled and a quieter and different kind of life awaited her?

Cade shifted closer to her and rested his hand on her shoulder. Always, her pulse skipped with his contact. Irritation rose inside her, not at him but at her own foolish reaction. He meant nothing. Cade's way approached what she would call a hands-on style, in the same way he trained a horse or dealt with the twins. A touch became his conversation.

"Am I boring you, Ally?"

Her head flew back. "Bore me? No. I'm thinking about the way we communicate—humans and animals. It's interesting. The slightest move has great meaning."

"It does with kids too. My girls know when I'm irritated without hearing me yelling. They see my back stiffen, my face tense, and they know. We are creatures of experience. We see it once and then again, and we understand. Have you ever trained a dog?"

"Here we go again." She arched her eyebrow.

"Ah, a poor example. But—"

"No, it's not. I'm teasing you. You're right. After a short time, a hand motion or one word sends the message to a dog, and he understands. He sits, he picks up what we drop, he shakes our hand. Dogs are smart. Have you ever trained a cat?"

His head flew back with a loud guffaw. "Never had the pleasure."

"They're harder to train, but they are trainable. I read an article about them, and it was interesting. I almost wanted to get a cat so I could train it. They'll do a high five, play drums or stringed instruments."

"And they read music?"

She gave him another arm poke. "No, but they like to perform if you give them a treat? Doesn't that sound familiar."

"It does which reminds me. Let's find some carrots for the horses."

She rose, happy to offer the horses a treat, but if she ever found that article on training cats, she'd make a copy and give it to Mr. Doubtful."

The treat Cade found became apples. She held one in the palm of her hand, and the horse did all the work. Once the fruit had left her hand, she enjoyed running her hand along the horse's mane or patting its withers.

"Ready?"

Cade's question brushed her ear. "Ready for what?" As soon as the words left she was sorry.

"You name it." He chuckled. "Follow me."

She eyed him a moment not sure what he had in

mind, but he strode ahead of her beckoning her follow and as she walked around the corner of the stable, she spotted Cade sitting on a swing."

"What have we here?" She sat beside him. "This looks like one of those old-fashioned porch swings."

"It was, but I rigged it up to hang from the tree. Not bad, don't you agree?"

"It's very nice." She pressed her back against the slats and stuck out her legs as if he would push them off, but instead the swing just moved in an easy sway. "Perfect."

"It is, isn't it?" He stretched his arm across the back of the swing, but it also touched her shoulders and the closeness turned her body to mush. A lengthy "ah" whispered from her throat as tension floated from her body.

"Relaxed?"

"Very." She turned her head to face him. "Thanks for the day, Cade. You make me happy."

"Likewise, Ally. You've come to mean a lot to me. I hope you know that."

Maybe she should have known, but her insecurity only created doubt and fear of disappointment. "I must have had a bad experience some time in my life, but I've blocked it. I never think of my presence in someone's life as being meaningful or special, Cade. Maybe that's why I'm always looking for the excitement. I hope one day it comes to me and I can put it to rest."

"You surprise me. I think of you as very sure of yourself, very confident. Am I wrong?"

She shrugged. "I don't know if that's really me or a front I put on to protect myself." She'd lowered her head, shocked that she'd shared that thought with him.

"Protect yourself from what?"

"Cade, I honestly don't know." She thought a moment. "Getting hurt, I suppose."

"Were you hurt in a relationship? I realize it's none of my business, but—"

"You're right, Cade, it's not your business. and it's something I don't talk about." She searched his probing eyes. "But I want to tell you this. I was engaged once in my late teens. I accepted thinking I could get away from my parents and their pitiful lives, but it took only a short time to know that marriage wasn't meant for me. Before we planned a wedding and I got in deeper, I gave him back the ring and vowed I'd never accept another proposal. Ever."

A dark frown washed over his face, and she was sorry she'd told him. That part of her life had been buried and resurrecting it could do nothing but damage. She saw that in Cade's expression. "I'm sorry, Cade. I didn't mean to be so blunt and negative."

"Ally, I asked, and you answered. I'm sorry I encouraged you to bring up something that you obviously wanted to forget."

"Never forget, but I can forgive myself and the poor guy I hurt so badly."

"You're not the only one who fears being hurt, Ally. I've been hurt badly once when Janet died, not only losing a wife, but being left with two three-year old daughters. Talk about panic. I was a walking zombie."

"I can't even imagine, Cade. I mean that. But you know, you've done an amazing job. The girls are as cute as can be, and though they are blunt and sometimes maybe too honest, they make me smile."

"Thank you. It's nice to hear you say that. And I hope you've noticed that I'm no longer a zombie. We can change, Ally. I learned that. It's not impossible. When things are right, it means an adjustment and that's it. It feels natural...even wonderful."

"I suppose some people can change. I've never felt that I could. I'm too...determined to do it my way." The Frank Sinatra song fluttered in her mind, and she couldn't stop her grin. "I sound like a jerk."

"No, you sound stubborn. I think that's the word."

"Thank you. I hate to admit it, but you're right."

"And that's something that can change too, Ally. I've already seen examples of that with you, and I'm not going to explain because then you'll be on your guard."

"Hey, this is my life. You should explain." She peered into his eyes, hoping he'd say what he meant.

"Maybe one day I will. Now you'll need patience."

"Wow. You know how to stop a woman in her tracks."

"Great. That's what I'm aiming for." His arm slipped from the swing back and slipped around her shoulders. "Ally, you make me smile."

She tilted her head upward to roll her eyes, but instead his warm lips touched her cheek, and all her eyes could do was close.

Cade straightened and swung his free arm in front of him. "Oops, I need to pick up the girls. Why not come with me? You can help me decide if this plan is going to work or not."

"You'll figure it out." She wasn't sure she could move.

He rose and took her hand. "Come on. It'll be fun, and maybe we could stop somewhere for dinner. How's that sound? Treats on me."

"Cade, you don't have to—"

"Correct. I don't have to, but I really want to. So, what do you say?"

A tourniquet had wrapped around her chest so tight, she feared she couldn't breathe. "I…" She got that out. "I should go home and—"

"And prepare dinner, but I'm doing that for you, so you really don't need to go home. Right?"

His warm smile and the playful look in his eyes captured her heart. "You're right. I'm your captive." And she meant every word.

"I'm so happy to hear that. Not only that I was right, but you're my captive. The girls will be thrilled to see you."

She gazed at him looking for his grin or something to let her know he was teasing, but she didn't see a thing. Only that glint in his gorgeous blue eyes.

Chapter 7

Cade pulled up at the church, and before he opened his door, the twins burst from the church, each waving something in their hand. He winked at Ally and slipped from the car to meet the girls. He noticed the registration woman in the doorway, and he waved so she knew who he was. She waved back, and before he could get his balance, the girls were on him.

"Look, Daddy." Chloe shoved the paper into this face and he had to grab it before it flew away on the breeze. "What is this?" He gazed at the drawing, recognizing the ranch and an improvised stick man wearing a cowboy hat with two girls close by and a woman between them. "His heart ached, positive they'd asked them to draw a family picture, and they didn't want to leave out their mom.

"It's nice, Chloe." He turned to see Jolie's. "What did you draw?"

She grinned and handed him her paper. "Instead of

outside, she'd drawn the family sitting around a table, with the same somewhat improvised stick figures, and their mom sitting with them. His chest ached for them.

"Jolie that's a great picture too. Are we eating dinner?"

Jolie frowned and pointed to the table. "No, that's not dinner. We're playing Old Maid. See, even Ally is playing too."

Ally. His pulse skipped, realizing his assumption had been very wrong. "Ally will like to see your picture, Jolie."

"Mine, too, Daddy." Chloe stuck the paper back in his face. "See, Ally is right here too."

"Yes, I see that, and if you look at the car, you'll notice someone in it."

Their heads shot up, and after a quick look, they spun around to face him. "Ally's here too."

Both girls darted toward the car before he could take a breath. Though relief swept over him, realizing they'd enjoyed their day at the church, yet their enthusiasm for Ally set him on edge. What would happen when Ally had enough of them and walked away?

He dragged himself to the car, needing to save Ally from the barrage of two eager young ladies, but when he got himself under control enough to get there, she had both girls trying to sit on her lap with their drawing jammed in her hand.

She gave him an odd grin as she admired each picture and commented on how nice they were to include her in the drawing. But in her eyes, regret and confusion shone like gems. She couldn't hide her true feelings, and the truth knifed his heart.

"Girls, you need to get in your seats with seatbelts hooked. Now."

From their looks, he got the message of you've-ruined-our fun, Daddy. He knew the look well. But despite their moaning, they did as he asked and settled into the backseat. He waited a moment until the two seatbelts were fastened.

"Where do we want to go for dinner?" He eyed the girls through the rearview mirror, but he'd first flashed a look at Ally.

"Anywhere, Cade. I'm not fussy."

The girls shouted out numerous choices, and then Junipers Grill came to mind. Thursday evenings they had a buffet. That way the girls could pick and choose and when they whined they didn't like what they picked they could go back and try something else. He couldn't help but grin at his plan. "How about Juniper's Buffet. They have good stuff, and you can see it before you put it on your plate."

"I like that, Daddy." Jolie jumped in first as Chloe tried to lean as close as her seatbelt would allow and raised her volume to get into the vote.

"Ally, what do you think?"

"As I said, I'm not fussy, and to be honest, I've never eaten there so it will be an adventure."

Her toying expression triggered a laugh. "And I know how much you love adventures."

She swung her arms his way and bumped his arm. "Watch it. You're making fun of my idiosyncrasy."

"I couldn't help myself."

"Daddy, it's not nice to make fun of people. That's what you tell us."

"You're right, Jolie. I made a mistake and I'm

sorry."

Chloe didn't want to be left out. "Tell Ally you're sorry, Daddy."

He flashed a quick wink at Ally and apologized. She accepted, and the girls finally leaned back and made their own conversation.

He lowered his voice, hoping not to be heard. "I also apologize for the other situation that upset you. I don't know how to tell them that—"

Ally reached across the distance and touched his shoulder. "Don't apologize for that. It's not that I was upset..." She whispered the word. "But I don't want them to get hurt. I don't know where my life is going. Who knows? One day I might move or...I don't know, I might do anything and then what does that do to the situation?"

Her words whacked against his chest, taking away his breath. He understood her concern and it made sense, but it's not what he wanted either and his own concern grew. Did she have something in mind? He wished she'd be honest if she had plans to leave the area or...or end their friendship. "I hope you think things through first, Ally, though it's none of my business, but as I said, you've grown on me, and—"

"I have no plans now, Cade. None. I want to be cautious. I've made mistakes in the past, and I don't want to do anything rash...or stupid. I will tell you if I'm giving thought to change."

"Thank you, Ally, and I mean that." He entered the roundabout and headed up the driveway to Juniper's Buffet. "It's a little early which means we'll find a parking space." His mind spun with all he'd heard from her today and he needed time to sort it out. Maybe he'd read more into her words than she meant, and maybe not.

"Here we go." He turned the wheel into a parking spot and turned off the engine. "Girls, you can unlatch your seatbelts, but listen to me. When we go in, I want you to let Ally or me dish up your choices. You're too short and the food will end up on the floor. Do you hear me?"

"Yes." An elaborated response reached him like a duet. Both girls at the same time unhappy with his request.

He opened his door, and before he rounded the car, the twins and Ally were on their feet and joined him, heading for the door. The restaurant didn't cater to children, but the girls were good eaters and he prided himself in the in-public behavior.

The hostess seated them at a table close to the window with a wonderful view of the golf course and the red rocks. They weren't too far from the buffet so that was a positive since the twins were with him. He could imagine them tipping their plates and sending their meal choices to the floor.

Before he sat, he suggested they pause for a moment while he checked the menu. Though the girls did their usually pouty acceptance, Ally agreed and settled against the chair back. He hurried away and moved through the buffet line, pleased that he spotted chicken, some kind of pasta and the dessert table offered the usual tempting choices.

He moved back to the table so the wait wasn't long, and listed off what he saw. When he mentioned the pasta both girls grinned and seem to be happy with the chicken. That was no surprise. "Girls, let me help you dish up what you want so we have no accidents, okay?" Instead of a response, he got their usual look, but that didn't bother him,

"I'll help, too, Cade. We won't hold up the line as much." Ally eyed the girls, and their faces glowed.

He could imagine the argument as to which one she would help, so he jumped in with a solution. "Okay, we'll trade off. Ally will do one of Chloe's choices and I'll do Jolie's and then we'll trade. Is that a good idea?"

Both girls grinned, their eyes glued to Ally. Though seeing the girls' enjoyment of Ally, the situation worried him as well. She'd been a good sport, but in the short time he'd known her, she'd made it clear that she wanted nothing to hold her back. Even a buffet would be slowed down by the girls' presence. But they were his daughters and he loved them.

He beckoned the girls to follow and when they rose, Chloe grabbed Ally's hand and ran off ahead of them. He followed Jolie, and as they approached the line with no one else there, gratitude filled his mind. The Lord wiped away his fears before they got hold of him.

Ally helped Chloe with a scoop of pasta, while he did the same for Jolie. The girls switched, and he handled the chicken. A few green beans made their plates and to his surprise, Chloe took some salad. Both girls wanted the buns. Once back at the table, he and Ally returned to select their food items, and for the first time since they left, he had a moment to talk with her.

"Thank you so much, Ally, for helping with the girls. I know this isn't your thing, but I do—"

"Cade, you don't have to thank me. I like the twins. They are typical of children who want to be grownup but aren't. I know you have your hands full at times, and I enjoy helping you with them."

"Really?" the question shot from his mouth before he could contain it.

"Really. I don't lie or exaggerate. You should know that by now."

He chuckled, as weight lifted from his chest. "I know. It's just too good to be true."

"But it is." She ran her free hand down his arm. "I'm not all grumpy and miserable if I don't get to have excitement or an adventure. In fact, those girls are a bit of excitement since you never know what will come out of their mouths." She gave his shoulder a pat and shifted to the next food choice.

So many things he wanted to say bundled in his heart, but this wasn't the time. All he could do was thank her, and that seemed so empty. He added salad to the meager empty space on his plate and set a bun on top of the baked chicken before he followed Ally back to the table.

"Can I have more pasta, Daddy?" Jolie leaned closer as if thinking that might influence him.

"Finish your chicken and some veggies and then I'll have a chance to eat my food before it's cold. Then we can go back to the buffet, but don't forget the dessert."

Chloe's head turned with the speed of a jet. "Is that cake?"

"It's cake and sometimes dessert bars with lemon."

"I like lemon." Jolie turned toward Ally as if wanting her to comment.

She didn't for a moment, but when she swallowed, she gave a nod. "I love lemon bars, and I notice that they have them."

"Yeah, we can have them together."

"We sure can." Ally gave her a wink and returned to her plate.

Cade watched with disbelieving eyes. He'd worried even before he'd told Ally about the girls anticipating how she would react, and since she met them, her attitude and kindness took away every concern he had. Ally showed nothing but warmth and tolerance. He could ask for nothing more.

♥

When Cade dropped Ally home from the restaurant, her head ached, and pressure weighted her lungs. Dealing with the girls hadn't been horrible, but she'd begun to learn how much time raising children could be, and it wasn't the life for her. The girl's drawings had made it worse. For some reason, she'd appeared in both girl's Bible school sketches of their family life. She'd only touched them in such small ways and yet her presence had made an impact.

Her emotions curled up and died when she saw what the twins had done with their pictures. They'd already lost a mother, and now they had drawn her into the family with their crayons, and one day she would no longer be there. She would vanish just as their mother had done. The cruelty knifed through her heart.

Now to make a decision, and the choice would be difficult. She could walk away before it became worse, stick around and try to let them know she was only a temporary friend...but a child of seven would never understand that. Or she could stick around and be the best friend she could be without a lifetime commitment.

She liked Cade. Liked him a lot if she were honest, and he liked her from what her instinct told her. He'd hugged her, put his arm around her shoulder, and kissed her cheek. What was next? And sadly, she had longed to kiss him on the mouth that day. She hadn't kissed a man in forever it seemed, and she often looked at Cade's lips, full and smooth like a ripe melon filled with a fresh taste and sweetness, arousing a longing she wanted to ignore but failed.

Her hand shot up to her head as the pain grew. She headed for the medicine chest and opened the Tylenol bottle, needing something to ease away the pressure. She'd been foolish to let things get this out of hand. Yes, she really liked Cade, but then his girls suddenly appear and that changed everything. What had been casual fun, a new adventure, horseback riding and enjoying his company had turned into a heartbreaking catastrophe.

Maybe she had gone over the top and blew the situation out of proportion, but looking in those little girls' eyes told her a different story. They liked her too much and had adopted her as a woman in their lives who could replace a bit of their mother. She plopped onto her recliner and leaned back, closing her eyes and trying to focus on anything but Cade and his girls.

Tomorrow, he'd offered another riding lesson, but she needed to think it through. She loved the horses and maybe in that environment, her mind would take her back to the first days they'd met and the fun she had without the emotional sensations that grew so slowly, they startled her when they came to life.

When the phone rang, she jumped and sat upright, her body tingling. She's fallen asleep which was a rare event for her. She rose and pulled her phone from her handbag. "Hello."

"Ally, I haven't been able to talk with you privately

except the short time at the buffet. I sense that you're upset with the girls, and I want to apologize. I know they take over our time together."

"Cade, that's not the problem, but I'm sure you see it. In the twins' imagination, I fear they see me as part of your family. I can't let that happen. They lost a mother, and I don't want to be the next person to walk out of their lives. It breaks my heart."

"I'm so sorry, Ally. I try to explain you're a friend, but I see that what I'm saying isn't sinking in. I can't tell you how many times, they ask me to invite you over so they can be with you. It's gone even beyond to play games. I don't know what to do."

"I think I do, Cade. I need to stay away for a while. Let them adjust now before it gets too deep and they are hurt. Let's forget the riding lesson tomorrow, and—"

"But they won't be home then, Ally, so you can still come for the riding. They won't know and—"

"Cade, I need to change for myself. I am attached to the routine, and I enjoy your company. You know that, but I also don't want either one of us to be hurt. Better to ease up now before it's too late." Too late? Too late for what? Her head whirred with unwanted emotions.

She waited but heard only silence. "Cade, are you there?"

A sigh eased over the phone. "Yes. I'm here, but I don't want to be."

Her stomach knotted. "I don't…I'm sorry then. I'll hang up, Cade, and give you a break." As she pulled the phone from her ear, she heard his voice. "Cade, did you say something?"

"I meant I don't want to be here at my house. I want to be with you, Ally. That's what I mean."

"That can't be. We've developed a pattern of how we spend time together and that has to be changed. For now, I'll stay clear of everything. Tell the girls I'm too busy at work and have some other things to take care of. They'll understand."

"They may, Ally, but I won't."

"You will when you think about it, Cade. I'm sorry but it has to be this way for now. Please try to understand." Instead of waiting for a response or more questions, she clicked off the phone as tears rolled down her cheeks.

She'd created a mess. If she'd stuck to her life style—fun and frolic—hot air balloons, rock climbing, hiking, experiencing new things…horseback riding…but she'd let her purpose slip and allowed emotions to become part of her life. She couldn't do that.

Brushing the tears from her eyes, she rose and headed to the computer. She loved riding the horses, so she needed to find another ranch, someplace else that would distract her. She settled into the chair, brought up a browser and entered horseback riding lessons in Sedona or Cottonwood, close to her work and handy.

She hit the button, and scanned her options, although the list surprised her since Cade Murphy's ranch didn't appear on the list. Thinking back, he'd never said his business was riding lessons, he mainly boarded horses and allowed experienced riders to use his horses by the hour. She'd manipulated the lessons.

Her headache shot a sharp pain down to her neck, and she rubbed the cords to ease the stress. Instead of thinking any more, she studied the list of ranches that taught riding. To her pleasant surprise, she saw Grif

Coleman's ranch on the list. That would work, and it would be a good distraction. Plus, she could spend more time with Marcy.

She shifted from the recliner to the sofa and stretched out. The pain killer began to kick in as her new plan eased her mind. She would call Grif from work tomorrow and see what could be arranged. If he asked why, she could mention that she didn't want to cut in to Cade's care of his girls. Her excuse sounded true and even thoughtful.

♥

Marcy studied her as they ate lunch together, obviously wanting to ask questions, but she didn't, and Ally didn't help the situation. "Marcy, have you ever considered taking horseback riding lessons?"

"Taking what?"

"You heard me. Riding lessons. I know you want to keep your feet on the ground, but they're fairly close to the ground when they slip onto the stirrups."

"Right." She shook her head and frowned. "Only a few feet away from the ground unless you're talking about a pony."

Ally let a whoosh of air leave her lungs. "No ponies. I'm talking horses."

"Are you tired of being alone with Cade? I can't believe that."

"I'm not taking lessons from Cade anymore. It's too difficult with the twins, and—"

"Come on, Ally." Marcy plowed her fists into her waist. "You can't fool me. I've known you for too long. What's happened?"

A lump settled in her throat as she tried to figure out what she could say to appease Marcy. "Nothing's wrong."

"Sure." Her tone added meaning to the single word.

"Okay, yes but it's not what you're thinking."

"And now you're a mind reader."

"No, but you think it's something to do with Cade, and it's not."

"Really? Then what's it to do with?"

"His girls. They're too attached to me, Marcy. They did a drawing at vacation Bible class of their family, and I was in the picture."

Marcy's eyebrows shot upward. "Are you sure?"

"Yes, I'm sure. They told us that the woman was me. Both girls did a separate drawing, and I was in both of them. Marcy, if I stay around and then walk away, I'm going to hurt those girls and I don't want to."

"I think it's too late, Ally. They care about you, obviously, and I'm sure their dad does too. You've been in their lives for a few weeks, and kids can gravitate easily to someone they find kind and friendly. I'm sure you were, even though you say you don't want children. I think you'd be a good mother."

"Me?" She poked herself in the chest. "You have to be crazy."

"Only a little."

Marcy's three words sprouted a grin on Ally's face without a warning. "I'm confused and sad, Marcy. I don't want to walk away from the kids. They're nice and even with their pouting ways, I can get a chuckle. They seem to think a pout will change the world, but it doesn't.

"Shoot! I'd planned to try that and see if it works for me."

Ally waved her words away. "Don't bother. It

won't."

Marcy's expression darkened. "So, what are you going to do? Can you really stay away from Cade?"

"Right now, I don't have much choice." A blip caught in her voice, and she swallowed the emotion rising from where she'd buried it. "I'll stay away for a while. Cade knows my reason and I hope he can explain it so it makes sense to the girls. Instead of lessons from Cade, I'm going to call Grif. He has a horse ranch too and offers beginning riding lessons, according to the Internet."

"Can that affect Cade's relationship with Grif?"

"Why would it?" Her empty response punched a hole in conscience, but she didn't want to face it. Staying away seemed all she could do.

Marcy shrugged. "It's your business, but don't ask me to take lessons with you. I'm not you, Ally. And thank the Lord for that."

At the moment, Ally could agree. She didn't want to hear herself bugging Marcy either. "I'll call Grif when we're done with lunch, that is if I have time. If not, I'll drop by the ranch after work and talk with him."

"Won't he be curious why you're doing this? I'm sure he knows that Cade's been giving you lessons."

"I'll be honest about the girls. He'll understand."

Marcy turned into a bobble-head. "I'm afraid he will, Ally, but not what you want him to understand."

She'd lost what Marcy meant, but she guessed she didn't want to know. Instead of responding, she turned her wrist to eye her watch. "We need to get back to work. Look at the time." She held her wrist in front of Marcy.

"You're right." Marcy took the last drink of her juice and set her soiled dishes on the tray.

Ally did the same, and they hurried to the tray deposit and headed back to work.

The day dragged which it always did when her mind burdened with confusion. Longing to empty her worries, she yearned to be outside so she could drive to Grif's ranch. Yet something held her back as she reviewed the idea. Perhaps she should call first. She had no guarantee that he was at the ranch. He probably had employees.

Though distracted, she made it through the day, and when the hour reached four o'clock, she said her goodbyes. Her shoulders lifted with her eagerness to get going. Once in the car, she gazed at her phone and weighed her options—call or not call. Taking a chance, she slipped her phone in her purse and started her car.

She'd checked Grif's address and figured she knew the general area. Using her GPS would have been wiser, but once again the old adventurer came out in her. Finding something on her own meant a bit of excitement. Her grin turned into a frown. Could she ever get rid of that ridiculous drive of doing something new and different?

As she approached the area away from the shops and businesses of Cottonwood, she drove along the highway with long vistas of green or dried brown fields with a mountainous backdrop. Eyeing the farms as she passed, her focus caught an arched driveway and the sign Coleman Horse Ranch buoyed her spirit.

She slowed and turned into the driveway where the fence had already been opened. She hoped that was a good sign. The stable seemed larger than Cade's and as she neared, she spotted two corrals where horses were nibbling on a haystack while others wandered aimlessly around the circle or settled down for a rest on the ground.

Though she expected to see a human somewhere in sight, none appeared. So, she continued forward and pulled up between the house and stable. When she stepped out, she spotted movement in the stable, so she headed that way, hoping it was Grif. The closer she got the more she realized it wasn't him.

The man looked up and faced her. "Can I help you?"

"I'm looking for Grif. Is he in?"

The man pointed toward the house, his expression growing to curiosity. "He's inside, I believe, but maybe I can help you."

She shook her head. "Thanks, but I'm sort of a friend and wanted to talk with him."

His expression changed while his eyes traveled up and down her length, making her ill at ease. "A sort of friend, huh?"

"I suppose a new friend I could say." She waved her arm toward Grif's home. "I'll just go to the house if that's okay."

"I guess. Suit yourself?" He didn't take his eyes from her.

Her discomfort grew as she turned to get away. She felt his eyes on her as she headed for Grif's door. She stepped beneath the overhang and knocked while a question surged through her. Should she mention the guy's weird behavior to Grif or let it go?

The door swung open, and Grif stood inside, surprise written on his face. "Ally? It's you, isn't it?"

"It is, Grif, and I'm sorry to just pop in. I suppose I should have called. I work in Cottonwood at Verde Valley Hospital, so I thought it was a good time to drop by and talk with you about a favor."

"A favor?" His head tilted as he studied her.

"Sort of, and I have good reason." She remained on the entrance slab and hoped she didn't have to explain the situation standing outside his door.

Regret washed over his face before a grin appeared. "Sorry. Where are my manners? Come in. I'm certainly not being a good host." He stepped back and beckoned her inside.

She stepped through the doorway into a large room filled with leather furniture in shades of brown and beige with art work of horses and desert scenes on the walls. "I can see a rancher lives here."

"I know. It's obvious a woman didn't help design this room."

"But it fits you, Grif. Perfect for a ranch setting. I like it." He'd motioned toward a chair and she ambled deeper into the room and sat. "How are things with you? Good I hope?"

"Very good. The weather's great for tourists, so the shop is selling well, and we've had numerous people stop here to ride horses. I'm always happy to see that."

"I'm sure you are." She paused to organize her thoughts. "And that sort of gets me to the topic. I know you rent horses for riding, but I also read that you give riding lessons. Is that true?"

His smile shifted to a sort of curious frown. "Occasionally, yes. I'm not doing as many lessons as I did once. It's time consuming teaching beginners. I don't mind working with seasoned horsemen...and women who want to ride. That's much less work for me. All most of them want is the use of a horse while a few want a few riding tips, but that's it."

"I see you have an assistant working outside."

"You mean, Buck. He's fairly new, but I needed someone to exercise the horses, keep them fed and to do everyone's favorite task of mucking out the stables." He grinned. "I take it you met him."

"Not formally, but he was curious who I was."

Grif released a long sigh. "I suppose I need to talk with him. He seems to enjoy checking out young women. I've heard that before and thought I'd made my point with him, but maybe I was too polite. He'll hear about it."

"Sorry, Grif. I didn't mean to make it an issue. I just felt a little uncomfortable."

"Anyone in his right mind can see you're a beautiful woman, Ally, but they don't have to gawk. One good look is all they need."

Surprised at his blunt response, she managed to monitor her reaction. "Thank you. Not everyone tells me that I'm beautiful. Have you had your eyes checked lately?" She grinned, and he grinned back. "No matter, it was nice to hear you say it." Instead of lingering on his comment, she needed to explain why she'd come.

"Grif, the reason I asked about the lessons might have confused you. You know that I had a number of lessons from Cade, but he's so tied up with the girls and..." Grif needed to hear the truth. "And I'm concerned about my involvement." She told him about their attachment, the pictures they drew and the situation that saddened her. "Those girls lost a mother, Grif, and I don't want them to put me in her place. I'm too much a free-spirit and—"

"Wow. Somehow, I had the idea that things were getting serious between you and Cade. Am I wrong? He talks about you so often, and I can tell how much he cares about you. I just assumed that—"

"You can't assume anything about me, Grif. I'm single by choice. I realized years ago that marriage and I aren't friends. I do care a great deal for Cade, and I really like the girls. Yes, they're over the top at times with energy and their blunt questions, but I've been able to laugh. Still I have no idea how that works long range, and that's one of the reasons I had to back off."

He studied her a moment in silence. "I knew you were spirited Ally, and I like that, but I have a hard time picturing you a mature woman without having had the joy of falling in love and having a family."

Her eyes widened. "Grif, look at you. You're single without marriage and family. Are you surviving?"

"Surviving, yes, but I question myself often, and lately I've begun to think that I might want to not only open my eyes, but open my heart. I think about a child calling me daddy, and I get a little twinge in my chest. That's a new sensation for me."

"Really?" His candor caused her to shake her head and she forced herself to stop. He didn't need to know how much he surprised her. "Sorry, but I hadn't anticipated your honesty. You seem more free spirited than Cade. I pictured you as a man who can stand on his own and love it."

"I have, but one day, I looked around the place, my little kingdom in Cottonwood, and asked myself who would be the one I'd leave this place to when I die."

"Die? I hope you're not saying…"

"No, I'm healthy as a horse, as they say…although occasionally horses do get sick." He grinned. "But I mean what will I leave behind besides this ranch. What legacy can I offer the world besides a house, stable and some horses?"

Legacy? Struck by the word, she stared at him, her mind reeling. "I suppose, at this point, my tombstone would read, 'Here lies Allysa Grant who lived for adventure and fun. That sounds empty doesn't it?"

He shrugged, as if hesitant to give an opinion. "It's how you look at it."

"I don't know, Grif. Once in a rare while, I ask myself what am I doing with my life, and then I let the question fade away. Maybe it's getting involved with Cade and the girls. I see two sweet kids who don't have a mom and hunger for a woman in their lives. It happens that they met me and I slipped into the niche they need." A lump caught in her throat, and she looked away afraid that tears might roll down her cheeks.

"You care about them, Ally. But I understand your concern. If you are sure you don't want to make a life commitment to Cade, then you're being wise."

"That's why I came to you about the lessons. I've had quite a few with Cade so I'm not a beginner. I was up to cantering, but I really want to get the experience of longer rides somewhere other than a meadow which is what we were doing."

"I know some great places, but I'd need to see you ride first. These trails go through forests, climb through the canyon and often cross the Oak Creek water. Can you do that?"

Her pulse palpitated. "I'd love it, but I would need your expert opinion. I always assume that I can do anything, and I'm not always right."

Grif let out a guffaw. "Glad you know who you are. We can give it a try, Ally, but I hate to hurt Cade in anyway. You know, he thinks—"

"I don't want to hurt him or the girls, Grif. I've already said that. If you're hesitant, I can look somewhere else, but—"

"Absolutely not. Some would have a tendency to accept the idea that you're a trained rider, and that could be a mistake. I'll do it for you. I won't take you on those difficult trails if I don't think you're ready."

"Good. That's what I want to know. Then maybe I could have more lessons."

He nodded. "When do you want to start? I could see you ride tomorrow after work, about this time. We'll go through some of the paces and see how you do."

"Perfect. Thanks so much." She stepped forward without thinking and gave him a hug. Grif stood like stone for a moment before he hugged back. "I didn't mean to scare you. I'm just very appreciative."

"You're welcome, Ally. I'll see you tomorrow then."

She rose and extended her hand. "Thank you so much, Grif."

"You're welcome."

She backed away and then turned to the door and stepped outside, hoping that Buck, the new guy, was off somewhere out of her sight. She darted to her car and pulled away.

Chapter 8

Cade's confusion sat in his gut like a huge rock. After going over and over his last few conversations with Ally, he made no sense out of her insistence to stay away for a while. His daughters liked her very much, and yes, they seemed to connect with her on a deeper plane, but all he needed to do was explain that Ally wouldn't always be there for them.

As the thought raked through his mind, a weight grew heavier in his chest. Why had he been led to a woman who wanted no part in commitment or even a long-term friendship? He'd been alone a long time. Four years without spending time with anyone had left him like a new teen boy in town having no idea how to get to know the girl next door.

Sadly, they weren't teens. They were adults watching years tick past. He'd loved Janet, but she'd been gone long enough for his arms to long to hold someone, his lips ached to kiss a woman he cared about, his empty bed had grown into a wasteland. How could a priest or monk live without the warm body of another person beside them at night?

Though he'd tried to deny his feelings for Ally, her disappearance dug truth from his soul. He cared about her more than a friend, even a good friend. He tried to keep his emotions under control, but his yearning grew even with Ally's blunt attitude about being a free, spur of the moment person who lived life for adventure. No matter what she said, nothing slowed his hope that one day she would discover that there was more to life than that.

Rather than see it herself, she'd walked away. The girls couldn't understand and insisted she would be back, but his flattened heart feared the worst. Her reasoning made sense and yet it didn't. If she really cared for him and the girls—loved them—she could never walk away. So now, he sat and stared into space, hope clinging to him like sticky syrup that he wanted to wash away.

One thing struck him. He'd never really courted Ally. She'd stepped into his life full of smiles and fun. She blended into his world, enjoyed the horses, admired the ranch, and seemed to enjoy his company. But she'd done that on her own. Maybe the time had come for him to become old fashioned and court her. But he had no idea how anymore. Courting was as old fashioned as the word itself. Even with Janet, they'd seemed to fall in love without an effort, one of those take-it-for-granted situations that had happened naturally.

How did a man court a woman? He knew how to ride a horse and be a father, but courting was beyond his natural ability and his knowledge. Maybe he needed courting lessons. Though he wanted to grin at the silly idea, he couldn't. He really needed to learn the art of courting.

♥

Ally left the hospital at the end of her work day after slipping on her western shirt. She hoped that might impress Grif. He was a kind man, different from Cade, but the same type of kindness. She liked him as a friend but that was it. He'd been open with her, which did surprise her when he admitted having thoughts of falling in love and marrying. His enthusiasm, though controlled, gave her food for thought.

A legacy. Hers was pitiful. When she was gone, what would she have left in this world as a legacy other than a few people's memories of her fun-loving nature, but that was rather pitiful even to her. People wrote books or poetry, created art work, made an impact on organizations or charities, designed clothing, homes or buildings. She'd done nothing like that but made a brochure that was handed out at the hospital. That would be updated eventually by someone else who worked the job.

As she settled into the driver's seat, a shiver ran down her spine. If Grif hadn't said the word legacy, the idea would have never struck her that she led a rather empty, non-useful life. When she was gone, everything relating to her would be gone. No inventions or creations, no husband, no children or grandchildren. Nothing.

She stared into space until it blurred from the tears in her eyes, and then pulled herself together and started the car. She left the hospital parking lot, today knowing her way to Grif's Since making the decision to avoid spending time with Cade and the girls, her days became as empty as she was. In her mind, she'd become a large pot on the stove with nothing in it. Useless. Empty, a cooking pot provided nothing for anyone when the potential was there. Fill the pot with water, beans and vegetables and she would be soup. Not now. The pot was empty. Filled with nothing.

Grif's ranch appeared ahead of her quicker than it had seemed the day before. Yet her spirit was brighter than the day before. She'd gone there with hope that he would agree to her lessons. Today, she might not care. What did her lessons offer the world or anyone but her own selfish need? The image turned her stomach.

As she pulled down Grif's long drive, a kind of sorrow covered her. How long had she lived wrapped in her own self-centered world? Yes, she'd learned to focus on patience and show them kindness, but beyond that, she'd accomplished nothing. The hot air balloon was a fun adventure, but what did it accomplish?

She needed to do more for others. One thing she could do was spend more time with Marcy, who tended to be a loner. Even though Marcy was pretty and a wonderful, thoughtful friend, she lived her life at home or work or occasionally did some volunteer work at her church. But nothing really for herself. Without much family around, she had a lonely life—no close friends other than her, and no man in her life.

Reaching a place to park, Ally rolled in and stopped the car. She spotted Grif near the stable, and concluded he was readying the horses for their ride—her test ride. She gave him a wave as she closed the distance between them. "Hi." She lifted her hand in greeting.

Grif gave her a nod along with a faint grin and

turned back to the horses. Taking good care of the horses defined the work of a good rancher.

When she reached him, she eyed the two horses he'd saddled up and knew immediately which one was her's to ride. It was a beautiful chestnut horse, its height less than the other horse he'd saddled, but the chestnut had a beautiful strong back from the hip line to the neck. She rested her hand on the horse's nose. "Is this one mine?"

"I thought you might enjoy riding a Morgan. He's well-trained and has a gentle temperament. He'll do what you tell him to do."

"I wish he could tell me what to do, but then that's not about to happen, right?"

He gave a playful snort and shook his head. "You're the leader here. He's the worker." He pointed to the wide open meadow. "We're going to head out to the valley for a bit until I have time to study your techniques and then we can try something more strenuous. Don't expect to climb mountains. Always use our sense when we ride."

"I got it." She gave the horses nose a rub and then paused. "What's his name?"

"Nothing too exciting. Because of his deep red-brown color, we call him Russet."

She chuckled when she felt Russet's head pull up. "He knows his name."

"He does. Depending on the tone of your voice, he can also understand what you want him to do." He shrugged. "But using your legs is probably a better method. Sometimes we use both."

"I remember that from my lessons. Thanks for reminding me."

"Are you ready? Although if your shirt is a sign, then I know you are."

"It's only a suggestion." She loved his smile. "I'm anxious to give it a try. I rode Bliss at Cade's, but none of the others. So, riding Russet will be a whole new experience."

"When learning to ride, one horse is probably best, but let's see how you do on Russet."

He patted the saddle as she eased her way toward him, keeping a brave face but inside surprised at her nerves. She'd been confident, but suddenly the new sensation caused her stomach to twitch and her spirit to sink.

Hoping with all the courage she could render, she slipped her foot into the stirrup and swung her leg over the saddle. She contained the joy she felt, not wanting to give her cowardly side away.

Grif's bright eyes gazed at her. "Ally, that was great. That shirt is not a suggestion. I think it's a sign that you're a pretty good rider." He shifted to the other horse, swung onto the saddle, and moved forward. "Bandit and I will move ahead in an easy walk, and then when you're comfortable, bring him closer."

He signaled Bandit and the horse moved off without a hitch. Reviewing what she had learned from Cade, she rested the reins in her hand, tightened her knee as she eased forward, while Russet moved forward in a gentle walk. Her confidence grew when Russet seemed to read her mind as she shifted an inch forward and as her knee tightened against the horse. He picked up pace, and in seconds she'd trotted ahead and passed Grif.

He got the point and soon he trotted beside her,

giving her a thumbs up with a grin. "Good job, Ally. Let's stay at this pace for a while as we get deeper into the meadow toward that grove of trees. Then we'll be near Oak Creek."

The creek. He'd mentioned that before and said when he had confidence that she could ride, they would cross the creek. Riding in water added an edge to the occasion, a new experience that she had always loved. An adventure. But today, not so much. She could injure herself and could deal with it, but she didn't want to injure the horse. That would break her heart. A little excitement wasn't worth it.

Her pulse skipped with her change of attitude and left her confused. Life had been a play land where she'd experienced many new activities from skiing on an Olympic trail, parachuting from a plane, rock climbing, parasailing, and the amazing experience of riding in a glider. She would never forget the landing, and yet when she thought of landing, the hot air balloon had been extremely scary but exciting. She loved it. Yet the joy she'd found lately was less dangerous and even more fulfilling.

She guided Russet beside Grif and glanced his way. He noticed her and slowed. She followed. "Sorry, I didn't mean to slow us down."

"You looked as if you had something to say."

She lowered her head before garnering courage to be open. "I guess I did. It's nothing really but thoughts running through my head."

"Then it's not nothing, Ally. It's thoughts you want to share."

"I guess it is." She first related her lifestyle, her driving personality to find excitement. "You may have heard that from Cade, but—"

"Cade isn't one to share other's thoughts, Ally. He often keeps those things to himself."

Her chest tightened picturing Cade's face. She missed him more than she wanted to admit.

"Thanks for telling me. I think I've learned something important. Adventure and fun aren't a life goal that's worthy. When we talked legacy, I realize that I want to make a change in my life. I'm startled to hear myself say that."

"Change can often be good. It's not a negative action in most cases. I'm glad you've discovered some things you'd like to improve…I think you could call it that."

"Yes, improve. Riding horseback has a purpose, an honest mode of transportation, and yet one that allows me to communicate with an animal in an amazing way. Getting to know and understanding horses helps me grow as a person."

"Ally, that's a meaningful awareness. I'm honestly happy to hear you sound so positive about the horse riding and getting to know the horses."

"Thanks, Grif. Through them, I've learned the importance of sensitivity and understanding. Offering the hard-working animal an apple or carrot, feeling their pleasure with the stroke of my hand is giving and not taking. For once it's not a selfish act, but one of kindness and gratefulness, a kind of thank you for the horse's hard work."

"Beautifully said."

His smile touched her heart. "I can't believe that this experience has been so dramatic. It's as if I've had a major life incident happen—like a serious car accident that I survived beyond everyone else's prediction. I'm talking about feeding a horse an apple or a carrot." The concept caused her to reel, and yet she meant every word.

"I know you're serious, Ally. I can see it on your face and hear it in your voice. Congratulations. Sometimes the simplest thing can arouse a life awareness followed by a change."

"That's right." She leaned forward, picking up Russet's pace, but Grif hung back as if he had more to say.

She slowed again until he was at her side.

"So, Ally, what are you going to do with the change? How will you use it?"

The question took her aback, and her uplifted spirit grew heavier. "I don't know, Grif. I need to give that some thought, but I hope it's something that's natural and not calculated."

"So do I, Ally, but I want you to think about it."

"I will."

Grif shifted forward and Bandit moved back into a trot, and she followed, seeing the creek so close she wondered how they'd gotten there, but then she knew. The conversation had grasped her focus like a vise.

Grif motioned to the water. "It's shallow over here. Are you ready to give this a try?"

She drew in a deep breath. "As ready as I'll ever be."

He gave a nod and Bandit stepped into the stream of water and headed across as she joined him, although concerned with every step that Russet would misstep and she would fall. As they climbed the bank on the other side, her audible sigh caught Grif's attention and he grinned.

"You made it and all in one piece."

"I like being in one piece. I'd prefer it that way."

He chuckled and then came to a stop. "Let's climb down and give the horses a rest and a chance to drink from the creek, and I brought along a treat for them."

She slipped off, as Grif dug into a small saddle bag that she hadn't noticed and pulled out two apples. He tossed her one and she held it while the two horses drank from the stream.

"Thanks for bringing the apples." She tossed hers in the air and caught it. "You're a good man, Grif."

"I appreciate that, Ally. And by the way, so is Cade. He called me recently and mentioned you."

"He did?" Her heart pounded like a wild drummer. "And he mentioned me? I hope he's not angry that I came to you for lessons."

"No. Nothing like that. He said he and the twins miss you. I think he's more confused than anything. He asked me if you'd told me what he'd done to make you leave."

"What he'd done? I tried to explain that the girls were liking me too much."

"Is that possible?" His gaze penetrated hers. "I suppose that's what he's asking himself. Most people are pleased to be liked."

"But... Grif, you know what I mean. I miss Cade and the girls. I just feared that they would get too attached and see me as a mother figure, and Cade might view me as one too...for the girls."

"So, you're saying that you never want to be a mother. Is that right, Ally?"

She closed her eyes, hoping to gather her wits. How

could she explain? "It sounds that way, Grif, but that's not exactly it."

"Then being a step-mother is your problem?"

"No, to be a step-mother means I have to marry a man who has children."

"Right. That's a fact. And what's the problem? Are you saying you have no feelings for Cade or perhaps, you don't like the girls."

"No, I do care about all of them. I…" She gasped for a breath as air escaped her lungs. "Grif, I don't know anything anymore."

"You are confused, Ally. Tell me why marriage frightens you."

His eyes searched hers with a look of honesty and interest, motivating her to tell him about her parents and her fears.

"For some reason, I trust you Grif, and I've told all of this to Cade, so he should understand why I don't want the girls to be hurt by my rejection of marriage and being their step-mother. The situation with my parents has blackened my view of marriage. I've never seen a good marriage in action, and I suppose that's why I am who I am."

As Grif's expression validated a sincere interest, she told him about her parents and their marriage made in hell, as she called it. Though he flashed a grin when she said it, the grin disappeared as if he did understand.

"I know, Grif, that somewhere in the world is a good marriage, but I'm a child of two people who should have never married each other. In fact, they should have probably never married anyone. What each wanted in life was what each wanted without consideration of the others' needs. They focused on their own wants and…"

Her breath drained from her, as tears misted her eyes. "And that's exactly what I let myself become, Grif. I have their genes, and maybe I will always focus on me and not a husband or family. That doesn't make a good marriage, and rather than take a chance, I'd rather save everyone from the pain of…"

Tears dripped to her cheeks while sobs broke from her throat.

Grif stepped beside her and drew her into his arms, her head on his shoulder wetting the fabric of his shirt. He didn't speak, but held her until her sobs faded. She gasped air into her lungs and lifted her head. "I'm sorry. I'm so sorry."

"Sorry for what, Ally?" He handed her a hanky he'd pulled from his pocket. "Awareness can be painful, but today you spoke words that you've needed to hear. You are basing your life on two people who fought like legendary Spartans. The battles were hard to win. But you knew that their way was not good. You've taken time to see that marriage is not a battleground but based on respect, love, cooperation and forgiveness."

"I wish I had your confidence, Grif."

"Give love a chance. Go back to what you left. Watch how you respond to the girls' needs and what you have done and are willing to do for Cade. If you can see that you're not just focused on yourself, but on them, then you'll know that you are not your parents. Your genes blended in a new way to create someone new. The Bible says, 'You are a new creation,' and you are."

She lowered her head, touched by his faith and his gentle nature. And yet how could he know or even guess who she really was inside. She didn't know. "Let me think about it, Grif. But thank you for listening and being by my side. It's great to have a friend like you."

"Ally, I'm sure you have more friends than you know. I'm guessing you haven't trusted those who've reached out to you, just as you've missed your mark with Cade and the girls. May I ask you a direct question?"

Concern ruffled through her chest. "What kind of question?"

"One about you. I think it will help your thoughts."

She weighed his request and nodded. "Okay, Grif."

"I ask this out of a fondness for you, Ally. But you need to ask yourself this. Do you like Ally?"

"Huh?" She drew her head back and pressed her lips together, irritated by the flutter in her stomach. "Are you asking if I like myself?"

He only nodded.

Her tongue dragged between her lips, wetting them so she could pry them apart. Her mind whirred with words, unable to sort her feelings and yet knowing that an answer should be readily available.

"I don't know." She dragged her fingers across her forehead. "I thought I did, but lately I've questioned what I'm doing with my life. You know. Our discussion on legacy and purpose. I need to think about that."

Without a comment, he drew the horses closer and fed them the apples. "We need to get back. It's getting late, but I do want to say that you did a good job today. Cade was a good teacher, Ally. And I believe, you were a good student. I wouldn't have brought you this far and crossed the creek without having confidence with your riding ability."

"Thank you, Grif, and thanks for your patience…and your concern about me. You've raised good questions, and we had a good talk. I promise to analyze all that we've discussed and the internal struggles I've been going through."

"I'm glad, Ally, and don't forget, Cade and the girls miss you very much."

She lifted her face to his. "And I miss them. Very, very much."

♥

Cade worked in the stable, listening to his girls' laugh as they ran around the yard playing tag or some game that resulted in an occasional giggle. Their laughter warmed his heart, but that was about the only thing that did in the past days.

Ally had become a part of his life, and he called her a good friend, but with her disappearance, he'd learned much more about himself and his feelings. He'd warned himself to not get involved. Life hurt when someone whom the person cared about walked away. He'd known Ally could do that, but he'd wanted to think she wouldn't. Well, he'd learned his lesson.

He leaned back against a stall, aware that he'd finished in there for the day, but time dragged without Ally breaking up his days with her silly adventure ideas. Though she'd slowed down on those, she still insisted excitement sat high on her list of experiences.

Children wanted excitement, but he'd never known an adult who still clung to the desire. And maybe that was part of her charm. Ally glowed with a joyful look at life and eagerness to be part of even the drudgery of life. He pictured her helping with the horses and loving them.

"Daddy." Jolie darted through the stable doorway with Chloe on her heels. "Guess who's here?"

"Grif?" He grinned at their enthusiasm. They liked his friend.

"No. Not Grif." Chloe danced around him. "Guess."

His pulse lurched with hope he'd tried to bury.

The girls spun around, and his gaze followed. "Ally."

"I know this is unexpected. I should have called, but you know me. I jump into action which can be good or bad."

He nodded. "I'm glad you came." As the words left his mouth, the twins dashed toward her, Chloe grasping her hand and Jolie cuddled to her arm.

"We missed you, Ally." Jolie's plaintive look broke his heart.

Chloe gazed up at her with a questioning expression. "Why did you go away?"

Ally crouched down and enveloped both girls in her arms. "Because I'm a bit goofy."

"Goofy?" Jolie's look changed from sadness to a grin. "Like Disney?"

"Not quite, but close. Sometimes adults do silly things that don't make sense, Jolie, and I'm sorry. I wish I could explain."

Her gaze lifted to his as his heart turned into a tom-tom. Words filled his head, but which to use escaped him. "We all missed you." He'd blocked out the other thoughts spinning in his mind.

Ally continued to hold the girls in her arms. "Can I start over again? Maybe I can make up for my—"

"Ally." He stepped closer, his gaze searching hers. "You don't need to make up for anything. Having you back here is what we want."

Moisture formed on her lashes and a few tears rolled down her cheeks. "Thank you, Cade." Her gaze lowered, shifting from one twin to the other. "Chloe and Jolie, you are wonderful girls, and I've missed you very much. Maybe now that I have my head back on my shoulders, we can enjoy time together."

Chloe searched Ally's face with confusion. "Where was your head?"

Ally grinned and gave her face a pat. "That only means that I wasn't using my head. It was there."

Relief washed over both twins' faces, and Jolie smiled up at her. "I didn't want to see you without a head either."

"Never. I think it's hooked on for good now." Her gaze shifted to him. "Cade, we can talk more later. Right now, let's do something fun...or I can help with the horses if you'd like."

He strutted beside her, longing to take her in his arms, but holding back. "You timed it right. Horses and stables are all taken care of so let's do something else."

"It's a beautiful day, but I'd rather do something with the girls. Could we do an easy walk around Bell Rock and Courthouse. Anyone up for that?"

The girls jumped up and down, relaying their delight in her suggestion.

Cade chuckled. "Girls, this is a fairly long walk for you and I'm not carrying you back, so I want you to put on your best walking shoes and be ready for a busy day. Then we'll go out and have something good to eat."

"Pizza." Synchronized response sailed from the girls.

He eyed Ally and saw her smile. "Pizza it is."

"If we're walking, then I need to get back and put on my walking shoes too." Ally shifted backward. "What time should I be back?"

"We'll pick you up. You're on the way. Is twenty minutes enough time?"

"Perfect."

He gave her a wink and watched her hurry to her car that he hadn't noticed earlier. But his girls had. They definitely had strong feelings for Ally, and though he didn't want to, their feelings worried him. Ally had good intentions, but no one knew when her intentions shifted to her wants. That would be brutal for the twins.

♥

Ally longed to talk privately with Cade, but that was one problem she couldn't solve since the girls glued themselves to her as they walked along the Bell Rock path. Her hope would rest on later in the evening, if Cade sent the girls to bed early enough. Maybe the walk would wear them out. That thought offered some optimism.

"Are we almost done?" Jolie's arms hung limp by her side and her enthusiasm had waned a half hour earlier.

Cade flashed Ally a look. "Not yet, Jolie. I know Courthouse Butte is harder to walk since you have to climb lots of rocks. But I know you both can do this."

She watched the twins faces distort from a sort-of pout to disbelief. Chloe glanced at Jolie and both sets of eyes widened.

"Daddy, I think your..." Chloe leaned closer to Jolie in a whisper. "What's that word?"

Jolie's face screwed into a question. "I don't know what word you mean?"

Chloe lifted her shoulders and let them drop. "You get better grades in English than I do, Jolie."

Ally held back her chuckle. "Do you mean the word expectation?"

Chloe's face glowed and she turned back to her Cade. "Daddy I think your expectation is too big. Jolie and I are tired already."

"And what did I tell you?"

They both gave him a blank look and shrugged.

"You have to walk, because I'm not carrying you back. You both wanted to come here, and so we are here."

"But…" Jolie's sad expression seemed to take her a few minutes to develop. "I'm really tired."

"Sit on a rock and rest." Ally pointed to a nearby outcropping. "It's probably easier if you turn around and go back rather than tackle Courthouse Rock."

"Can we daddy?"

Cade grew heavy lidded, as if try to hide rolling his eyes. "Girls, you can go back, but follow the path that we came on, do not talk with strangers and wait for us as soon as you see the path to the parking lot. We'll meet you there soon, or maybe we'll beat you there."

Ally doubted that. This part of the walk meant trudging up layers of rock and that could be tricky even for adults. She should have been using the walks for exercise and getting her legs stronger to climb without being miserable. In fact, turning around almost sounded good to her.

But Cade kept moving forward, and being the person always looking for a challenge, she had to keep her mouth shut. She hurried ahead, and when she caught up with him, she longed to talk about the things that had been in her mind and heart, but Cade looked thoughtful—probably worried about the girls—so she didn't bring up any of it. Hopefully, a time would come later.

"Do you want to pick up our pace, Cade?" She hoped she had the stamina, but his concern showed on his face.

"If you can. I shouldn't have let the girls go back by themselves. I assume anyone walking around these trails have nothing bad in mind. Kidnappers don't usually hike in popular places like these trails."

"They'll be fine, I'm sure, and if you want, I can hurry back and walk with them."

"Thanks, but no. I'm just being silly. They'll be okay."

She moved alongside him and only stepped ahead or back if others came along who wanted to pass them. He did step up the pace, and somehow, she managed to stay close to him. He'd been wise to send the girls back. Bell Rock was basically flat with no rugged rocks, but the additional path did have some layered rocks rising to a higher level of the butte and even she had a difficult time with some of them.

As they turned, she looked ahead and could see the cars parked a long distance away, and she relaxed though anxious to see the girls waiting for them. Her worries were soon over when she spotted the girls hurrying to meet them. She opened her arms and both girls ran into her embrace.

Cade's smile warmed her as he stood back and eyed them hugging on the path. "Where's my hug?"

Jolie was the first to break free and dart into Cade's arms, but Chloe stayed a moment longer, gazing into her eyes as if she were reading a good book and hated to walk away from the plot. Finally, Chloe let go and gave her dad a hug too. "Can we eat now?"

He tousled her hair. "No, I thought I'd let you starve."

Chloe pulled back. "Daddy, are you mad because we—"

"Whoa, there. I'm not mad. I'm teasing you."

Jolie gave him a poke. "We're not horses, Daddy. You said whoa."

Ally couldn't help but chuckle since she'd thought the same thing, but she didn't admit it.

The four of them joined hands on the path back to the parking lot—Jolie holding Cade's hand, Chloe holding hers and Cade guided his fingers through hers as they walked side by side.

Cade had never held her hand before. As close as he'd gotten was to help her off the horse when she had one of her first lessons. His hand around hers and feeling Chloe's smaller hand against her palm caused her heart to swell.

She'd never really experienced the sense of family, not like this, and today she knew what it meant. A bond, a kind of closeness sent a sweet warmth through her body, a sensation she'd never encountered in her lifetime.

With pizza on their minds, the girls talked so much on the way to Pago's that she didn't even try to carry on a conversation with Cade. Her hope clung to later in the evening. Maybe then, she could tell him what she'd learned in her days avoiding him and the girls.

Chapter 9

Cade turned off the lights and stepped from the twins' bedroom. His concern rose when Ally became too quiet. She'd spent time on the walk with few comments, and even at the restaurant her comments focused on the good pizza, and conversation with the girls, and even without asking him to join, them, they'd played a game of Old Maid. He'd turned into a third wheel…maybe fourth. The silly thought brought out a grin, one he needed.

Ally waited for him, her head resting on the sofa back, her eyes closed. He'd been grateful that she'd chosen to come to the house rather than have him drop her off at home. She said she didn't mind walking since it wasn't far. But he still hated her to walk home alone.

She looked up as he neared her. "Girls asleep?"

"Not quite, but they'll be sleeping shortly. The exercise wore them out, so I had faith that the bed would look good to them tonight. I think I'm right."

She gave a nod. "It's been nice being with them today, Cade. They are very sweet and loving girls, full of energy…except for walking around Courthouse." She grinned. "You can be proud of how you've raised them."

He settled beside her on the sofa and slipped his arm across the back. "Thanks, Ally, and playing Old Maid topped the day."

He drew her closer. "Losing their mom at that early age dragged me in a whirlwind of fear. How do you explain to children that young that their mother is in heaven? They don't understand, and failure weighted me down like a collapsed building. I had nowhere to turn because I didn't want people to tell me I was doing great. I wasn't. And even talking with my parents meant upsetting them."

"I can't imagine, Cade. But whatever you did, you did a great job. They are happy, smart, funny, and dramatic as girls can be. I love seeing them in action."

"But if they talked less, it might be a nice attribute." He gave her a wink. "I know you had things to say. I've learned to read your face, and it's easy to get frustrated when you'd like a few minutes alone to hold a conversation."

"I can't deny that, Cade, but I managed to be patient which for me is a miracle. A few months ago, I think it was impossible."

"Really?"

"You know my philosophy—have fun, find excitement and adventure, live spur of the moment—and don't let anything or anyone stop me." She looked away not wanting to see his reaction. "But something has happened. I've had time to think and time to weigh life, purpose, and legacy…a word I learned from Grif."

"Grif?"

She lowered her head as if uneasy. "Yes, Grif." Her expression saddened him. "I hope you understand, Cade. You know I took more lessons from Grif although he said I didn't really need lessons, just more experience. He acknowledged that you were a great teacher. I agreed."

"Thanks, but teaching you was easy and fun."

"It was." She drew in a ragged breath. "Cade, I don't want you to misunderstand what I'm going to say, but—"

"Ally, are you saying goodbye?"

"Goodbye?" She searched his face, his eyes filled with concern. "No, the opposite. Hello."

"Hello?" His head spun. "Are you saying that you want to be friends even though I'm a dad with two precocious daughters."

"Even then, Cade. I haven't experienced a miracle, but I have had time to think and to ask myself many questions. Maybe I can explain."

"I would love to hear about it." He shifted his arm from the sofa back and lowered it to her shoulders. Instead of drawing away, she smiled.

"Grif told me that recently he's been concerned about what would happen to his ranch when he was gone. He has no one to leave his legacy, as he called it. As he talked, my own lack of legacy struck me hard."

As she talked, he began to understand, and his interest rose in her revelation.

"Cade, can you see why I finally realized that a person can have some fun and new experiences, but it's not what makes life worthwhile?"

"I think I understand. We all want to leave something good behind when we meet our maker."

"Yes, and I had nothing to leave or to be remembered for. My head spun, Cade, when I faced that truth. I spent my life talking about every new experience I've had, but it never dawned on me that what I had was over—gone and only a memory. And sadly, only my memory, not even one that I shared with someone."

He studied her tense face. "So, what will you do now?"

"I'm not sure. I hope that you can help me, you know, as a friend. I want to live in a way that I accomplish something that lasts and not those fleeting events that are gone."

"I'm not sure how I can help you, Ally. I don't do much but take care of my horses and the stables and raise my girls."

She pulled back, her jaw dropping. "Did I hear you say you don't do much? Are you kidding?" She shifted on the cushion to face him. "You're raising two seven-year-old girls alone, Cade. On top of that you run a ranch that provides not only pleasure for many people, including me, but provides you with enough income to have a lovely and secure home. How can you say you don't do much?"

Along with a shrug, his fingers cupped around her shoulder as one finger brushed her flesh. "You see more in me than I do, Ally. I guess I take all that for granted."

"It's time to be pleased at what you've done, Cade. I'm getting a late start, but I need to find what my life was meant to be, too."

"Ally, you have an important job helping people who've been ill. You provide guidance for them and let them see that you care. That's an amazing gift to those who have gone through health trials and dealt with fear and worry."

Air drained from her lungs. "I guess you have a point, but I've never thought of my job that way. It's one of those 'someone has to do it' and that's what it's been to me."

"But you have training, and you've created information for them to take home that will guide them. Don't belittle that talent, Ally. Not everyone could do that job."

She pressed her hand against her chest. "You've humbled me without realizing it, Cade. I've never thought of my work in that light, and maybe you're right. Sometimes I get numerous thank yous from families for the time I spend with them and for the brochures I give them. But I still never, never saw it that way."

"You see it now."

"But I want to add to that, Cade. I admire what you do. You have a career and a family, and you do an amazing job with both of them. I'm lucky if—"

"You're still young, Ally. Life isn't ending tomorrow for you. Give it time and thought. You'll realize one day what it is you were meant to leave as your legacy. I hope I'm there to enjoy it with you."

She closed her lids, and when she lifted them her eyes connected to his and he drew closer. Today, he would take a chance, one he'd long to act on for weeks.

Her gaze lowered to his mouth, and the look let him know that today she had no intention of stopping him.

His lips parted as he lowered them to—

"Daddy." He jerked back and twisted his neck to face the voice.

Ally's head jarred the same as his had. Chloe moved from the hallway door and closed the distance between them. "I can't sleep right now, and I want to stay up and be with you and Ally."

Cade lowered his arm and rose, trying to focus on Chloe while his mind clung to the kiss he'd missed with her interruption. "My sweet daughter, it's bedtime for people who are seven. Ally and I have spent the whole day with you, and right now, we're talking and enjoying the quiet."

"But you weren't talking. You were looking at each other…real close." She dragged out the last two words.

Ally pressed her lips together, no doubt to muffle a laugh, and he wished he could have muffled Chloe. "I was looking in her eyes."

"Did you have something in them, Ally?" Chloe stepped closer, her eyes studied Ally's

"Maybe, but your daddy didn't find anything there."

He contained his amusement as Ally stuck to the truth while avoiding details. He rose and ambled toward her. "It's time for bed, Chloe, and this time, I want you to stay there."

"But what if—"

"If there's an emergency, you and Jolie will be the first ones I rescue. Now, for the last time, go to bed."

Ally's whisper brushed his ear. "I'll read them a short bedtime story. What do you say?

He eyed her a moment and nodded. "Chloe, Ally's going to read you a short bedtime story and then if you close your eyes, you'll be asleep in no time." He glanced at Ally, and she rose and guided Chloe to the bedroom.

Cade sat on the sofa, calming his irritation, but then regretted it. Ally had chosen the sweetest way he could think of to send the girls to bed. He hadn't made a good mother but Ally would be, despite her fears that she would not.

When he heard the bedroom door close, he smiled "Everyone okay?"

She closed the distance between them as she whispered. "Could be better. They both fell asleep before I finished the story."

Cade chuckled as he patted the spot next to him. Though the situation had ended, he still was nudged by disappointment at Chloe's bad timing. The twins seemed to have a talent for walking in on what would have been special moments. "Let's whisper, just in case."

Ally pressed her hand to his cheek. "They're curious, Cade. I'm guessing I'm the first woman who's been hanging around the ranch since Janet died. Am I right?"

"You are. It's been years since a woman has caught my attention. During that time, I had women let me know that they were available, but what they didn't know is that I wasn't...not until recently." He touched her cheek, the softness tingled against his fingers. "Can we roll back the clock?"

The question covered her face for a moment, and then she appeared to understand. "Yes, let's back up a few minutes."

He settled beside her, his arm around her shoulders

where it had been, while his eyes searched hers. His chest quaked like a washing machine, but he ignored the sensation, and lowered his mouth closer to hers, his lips parted when they touched hers. She trembled as her mouth moved beneath his and his own body, like a piece of ice, melted.

A soft moan slipped into the air, and he eased back, hoping her response represented a positive reaction. "I hope I didn't—"

"Cade, you did nothing wrong. To be honest, I was disappointed when Chloe stopped you the first time."

He wrapped his hands around hers. "So was I. My girls seem to have bad timing."

"Maybe not. It was worth the wait." She leaned closer and brushed her lips across his. "I had a negative attitude about kids, as you know, Cade, before I met your girls. I realize that things don't always go as planned when you have to make two young ones happy or pay the price."

He chuckled. "They do know how to raise the cost."

"They do, but they also add a spark to life. You never know what will happen next."

"You have that right." He squeezed her hand. "I'm so happy you didn't give up on us entirely, Ally. I understand that it's a shock meeting someone you think is as carefree as you are, and then learning that it's not so...and then realizing that what you learn is even more complicated than you could ever imagine."

"But you know I like challenges." She brushed her palm across his cheek.

He laughed in full agreement. "You do, and I'm sure we can provide challenges. Lots of them."

Her smile faded, replaced by a vague expression. "I

had a few things to talk about with you when we were alone. But it's late, Cade, and it's nothing bad, just thoughts I had when I was away. I'll see you tomorrow after work if that's good for you."

"It's fine as long as you—"

She touched his arm. "Cade, please. Don't worry that I'm going to walk away again. I'm not. I promise."

He clung to the hope that her promise would hold up. He'd fallen in love, and he could only pray that she had done the same.

♥

The memory of Cade's kiss clung to Ally's mind through the night and lingered in the morning as she talked with patients, but as she worked, Cade's advice touched her. He had been correct about her work. She found it easier to focus more attention to her job than she'd had in the past…really focus. The care of patients which she had taken for granted now became far more like a gift to the patients and their families. She could read the gratefulness in their faces. Her awareness added spirit to her work, enthusiasm, focus, and true concern.

When she met Marcy for lunch, she admitted what had happened, and Marcy's expression validated the new attitude she'd begun to experience.

"You mean you never realized the importance of your work? You're one of the last people at the hospital to send them off with hope and helpful information that gives them confidence. You validate that what the doctor said was true—the patient is on the road to recovery. Or the patient has a long way to go but recovery is possible. Those things mean a lot to people who've been living with worry and fear."

Ally stared at her soup bowl while her mind filled with tangled thoughts. "I've been negligent, Marcy, negligent of my life and my purpose. I talked with Cade about my wasted time, thinking fun and adventure was life's all in all. It's not. Relationships are that, and I mean all kinds of relationships. Patient to doctors and hospital staff, sister to sister, friend to friend, man to woman, husband to wife, parents to their children."

"Cade's rubbing off on you, Ally." Marcy reached across the table and cupped her hand.

"Grif helped me see all of this, Marcy. He's a great guy, and I respect him very much."

She drew back. "You're talking about that other rancher, the friend of Cade's?"

"Yes, he's the one that I asked to continue the riding lessons, except he said all I needed was more experience and so that's what we did. We road across the vast fields. I even forged the creek on horseback."

"You're not getting interested in—"

"In Grif? Not at all. I respect him and like him, but it's not that kind of relationship. He did admit that he's led a single life and now realizes what he's missing." Her heart skipped as she gazed at Marcy. "Grif said he'd like to meet a good woman and fall in love. He wants to get married."

"Ally, are you sure he wasn't suggesting that—"

"No...he's not interested in me. He knows I'm close to Cade, and he would never attempt to lure me away. It wouldn't happen anyway, but Grif's an honest and kind man. He just admitted that he has no one in his life and everything he does will end when he dies. He wants to leave a legacy."

"A what?"

"You know, leave something behind that will make a difference. His ranch and horses will be sold when he dies. They won't be connected to him unless he has children to leave it to. Think about it."

"I suppose he's right. Does he have a brother?"

She shook he head. "I don't know, Marcy, but he wants more in his life…not a brother."

Marcy's eyes widened. "Okay, I got you."

"Good. Think about it. You and I don't have legacies either. It's made me think…a lot." She reached out and pressed her hand on Marcy's shoulder. "You need to think about it too. Get out in the world and meet people. You're like a hermit, Marcy. You're such a great person, but you don't let anyone know."

Marcy grimaced. "My parents told me to be seen and not heard. I decided to do both. Not be seen or heard. Life's easier that way. I do my job here at the hospital. I do some gardening." She lifted her eyes to Ally. "You know that. I watch TV. I go to church. I have lunch with you."

"Yes, you do a few things, but you're so much more than that. Please think about what I'm saying."

Marcy lowered her eyes as if studying the design in the table. "Okay, I'll think."

"Let's have some fun and go to Flagstaff or Prescott and do some shopping. Buy a new wardrobe, get your hair styled a different way. We can both use updating."

Though she grinned, Marcy only stared at her. "I'm sensing that you mean—we can both use dating. Forget the up part."

"Okay, that too."

"I'm not ready for that, Ally. Really."

"But you will be after we get a makeover, you

know, new hair styles, some new clothes, maybe take a class in applying makeup."

"Okay, now you're going too far."

Ally grinned and yet suspected she could use all of that too. "We'll see."

♥

After work a kind of excitement revved Ally's spirit with so much to tell Cade about her work and about them. When she arrived at the ranch, she spotted the girls outside playing with a dog and it roused her curiosity. She hurried to the front door, gave a knock and opened it. "Cade?"

"I'm here, Ally." His head poked out from the corner of the archway. "I'm looking for recipes so the girls can make cookies. They keep asking and the cookies I serve are found in a box or cellophane wrapper."

She grinned and joined him in the kitchen. "I saw them outside with a dog. Don't tell me you went out this morning and bought—"

"No." He raised his had to stop her. "The neighbor is going out for the day, and their dog gets antsy when left alone for a long time, so they noticed the girls playing outside and asked if they could leave the dog with us until after dinner."

"That was kind." She moved closer and touched his cheek. "You're a good man, Cade Murphy."

"Thank you." He gave her a head nod. "But you're better than good. You're wonderful."

"You can't fool me. You're trying to coerce me into helping with the cookies." She grasped his arm and drew him to face her. "Am I right?"

Instead of a response, he drew her into his arms, and

his lips met hers. Her knees melted like hot wax on a candle, and she clung to him as if hanging on to life. As he eased back, she caught her breath. "Evasive, yes, but it worked. I'll help make the cookies."

He nuzzled her neck as he chuckled. "I can't tell you, Ally, how you've changed my life. I never thought that someday I would find a woman who—"

"Willingly baked cookies for you."

He burst into laughter, and she joined him. "Here's the deal. I have a recipe that is so easy to make. Just tell me that the girls like peanut butter."

"They love it."

"Good. All we need is peanut butter, brown sugar." She lifted her gaze, and he nodded. "One egg, and baking soda."

"Ready and waiting." He shifted away and pulled out all the ingredients she'd mentioned from a cabinet and then opened the refrigerator for the egg. "Are you sure? What about flour?"

"No flour, so it's also glutton free and less calories than some cookies."

"You're amazing, Ally." He opened a lower cabinet and pulled out a bowl. Together they measured and mixed until the dough was ready for the oven.

Cade drew her into his arms. "I'm guessing the scent of baking cookies will float out across the field and the girls will suddenly appear."

"That wouldn't surprise me. It bakes for only about 10 minutes, so keep your eyes open."

He sank onto a kitchen chair and pulled her onto his lap. "Getting serious, Ally. I realize we haven't known each other a long time, but somehow, I feel I've known you forever. The good and the bad."

"Ah, so you're telling me I'm not really wonderful now. I'm bad."

"But it's the kind of bad I can handle and the wonderful part shines."

She chucked him under the chin. "Sweet talk doesn't fool me." But she loved it and lowered her lips to brush his with a quick kiss. They sat in silence, her head on his shoulder, until the buzzer reminded her of the cookies and she jumped up.

She darted into the kitchen and opened the oven, happy to see the cookies were golden brown. She pulled them out and set them on a cooling rack before returning to the living room. "We should tell the girls we have warm cookies."

He grinned at her as she headed to the door.

When she stepped outside, she turned in the direction they had been earlier, but they weren't there so she headed toward the stable. They enjoyed the horses as much as she did—and that still surprised her how they had captured her interest.

As she stood in the stable doorway, she strained her eyes and saw nothing. "Chloe?" She moved inside, still hearing nothing. "Jolie?"

Silence.

The dog should bark or run toward her, but the only thing she heard was the movement of a horse and a soft whinny as if expecting a treat. Her chest tightened as her heart smacked against her breast bone. Something was wrong...or was she just overly concerned. She'd never had children, and she suspected seasoned parents would chuckle at her distress.

Instead of panicking, she left the stable and wandered back toward the corral where a few horses were resting or ambling around the circle. No sign of the girls could be found, and she turned in a full circle looking toward the meadow and the rocky background. No girls. No dog. Her pulse clipped through her body, and she hurried back toward the house, fearing the worst.

As she approached the doorway, Cade stood behind the screen, and when he saw her, he stepped outside, tension growing on his face. "What's wrong? Can't you find them?"

Tears blurred her eyes as she managed to respond. "I don't see them anywhere."

He hurried toward her. "Where did you look?"

She told him what she'd done. "I looked toward the fields and saw nothing. When I called their names, I thought the dog would respond, at least, but nothing."

He darted past her toward the stable, and she followed, concerned and surprised at the emotions knotting her chest and her mind. Were they lost? Could they be hurt? Questions and fears spiraled through her head.

Cade charged into the stable, and when she dashed inside, he had tugged a saddle off its stand and settled it on Dixie. "Ally, would you get the tack ready, and I'll saddle Bliss for you. I'm guessing you want to go too."

"No guessing, Cade. Definitely." She did as he asked, grasping the bridle and reins while he saddled up Bliss for her.

In moments, they trotted out of the stable and cantered into the field heading toward Lee Mountain. As they rode, she searched the horizon as did Cade. The further they rode, the more desperate she became. Where would the twins go? Why? In the back of her mind, images of bobcats, Javelina, and mountain lions grew out of proportion. Rattlesnakes loomed beneath rocks and slithered from grassy fields. Her chest ached from the pounding of her heart.

Cade's eyes didn't veer from the landscape. He turned toward the hills and then back to the horizon, both of them longing to see something to give them hope. His head lowered, and he spoke but she could barely hear him. "They've never done this before."

"Something happened to make them leave the ranch, Cade? Do you think the neighbors returned and they went down the street with them to be with the dog?"

"No, they would have told me, Ally. The girls always tell me where they're going."

His certainty deepened her fear. Kidnappings happened, but...two girls didn't make sense to her. "We'll find them, Cade." Her mind jogged with possibilities, anything that would make sense, until she wanted to scream. "Do you know the dog's name?"

"Spike. Why?"

"Let's call the dog's name. If he hears it, he'll bark or come this way."

"This is a lot of open land, Ally. I'm not sure the dog would hear us."

"But we can try." She lifted her hand and circled her fingers around her mouth. "Spike." She waited a moment and tried again.

Finally, Cade's deeper voice bellowed the dog's name. They waited and listened but heard nothing. "It's hopeless."

"Nothing's hopeless unless we give up, Cade." Picturing the girls alone in the huge field sent gooseflesh rippling down her back. Something had caused them to wander that far, but what happened hung in her mind like a loose thread.

"Let's head toward the mountain. Maybe a mule deer or elk wandered into the field and the dog saw it. If he ran toward it, the girls might follow, and the elk would high-tail it back to the mountain. I'm guessing the dog would follow along with the twins."

He said nothing for a few moments, and then reined the horse left in the direction she'd suggested. He picked up pace and she managed to stay beside him, praying she hadn't misguided him. Yet a sense of certainty filled her head.

As they neared, she cupped her mouth again, blasting as loud as she could. "Chloe. Jolie. Spike." Her hope lessened, and sorrow grew in her heart. She slowed and Cade road up beside her.

"I have to believe they're okay, Ally. I wish the Lord would give us a sign, but..."

"They're fine, Cade. I feel it in my heart." But her stomach didn't feel it as fear knotted in her belly.

Cade tilted his head back to the mountain and as he did, he paused. "Do you see that?" He pointed to the right away from the mountain.

She followed the direction of his finger and saw a spot of bright color caught on a weedy patch. "What is it?"

"A ribbon, I think."

"Yes, I noticed they wore them on their ponytails when I arrived. Thank the Lord, one of them lost one."

"And they rarely have ponytails, but they did because of playing with the dog." He nudged his knee and Dixie trotted in the direction of the bright color.

She joined him, and when they reached the spot, Cade jumped from the horse and picked up the bright bow. "This is it. They've been here."

"Maybe they're going toward the mesa, Cade and not Lee Mountain."

He looked toward Wild Horse Mesa while a frown grew on his face. "You might be right. I'm guessing there could be more wild animals on the mesa than the mountain. Let's go."

Before she could collect her thoughts, Cade tugged Dixie's reins, and she cantered ahead, her gait growing faster than Ally had ever seen.

She pulled the reins and Bliss understood as her trot turned to a canter, but Cade had pulled ahead and she wasn't sure she had the skill to keep up.

When he realized how far behind she'd gotten, he slowed. "I'm sorry, Ally. I'm so worried, and I realize you've never used the tolt gait before. A horse can go twenty miles an hour with that gait."

"Twenty miles." Her eyes had widened as she gaped at him. "I don't want to hold you back, Cade. Go on ahead. I can see you and follow. Please."

His eyes searched hers, and the fear radiated to her heart. "Please. I know you're worried. These rocks and hills can be the home of bobcats, mountain lions, Javelina, elk, mule deer, and who knows what else. Please go ahead or I'll turn back and wait for you there."

"Ally, you're an amazing woman. I see in your face that care about the girls, and—"

"Cade, I love your girls."

His gorgeous blue eyes misted as he turned away and headed across the field. She followed as best she could, and Bliss wanted to keep up, so she wasn't that far behind.

Mingled with the horse's hooves, her chest tightened when she heard a sound in the distance. A dog bark or maybe a coyote, but she prayed it was Spike.

Cade heard it too, since he dug deeper into Dixie's sides and the horse flew on ahead while Bliss made an attempt to stay as close behind as she could.

The sound grew closer and she searched the landscape, praying to see a flash of color, the red ribbon still on one of the twins or their colorful tops. Cade looked like a miniature toy cowboy so far ahead of her, but that's what she asked him to do. The girls were precious and holding back for her lack of skill would have broken her heart.

When Cade seemed to grow closer, she realized he had stopped, his head tilted upward, and when she raised her eyes in that direction, she saw a flash of color. Tears rolled down her cheeks, tears of joy. Certain that he had foundthe girls, she dug her knees into Bliss and clung to the saddle horn, praying she would not lose balance and fall off the horse's back.

Cade had turned to face her his hand pointing upward. She nodded, and soon she'd reached him and could see what he had seen, Jolie, Chloe and Spike high up on a rock that jutted from the mesa. Panic filled their faces, and their situation became clear. They'd gotten that far and couldn't go up or down.

She slowed Bliss and joined Cade on the ground. His arm slipped around her shoulder as a tremor rolled down his body. "The girls can't get back down, so I'm going up to see what I can do."

"I'll stay here, and if you need professional help, let me know. I can call 911 and explain."

He didn't disagree, and with a nod, he gave Dixie's rein a light tug and she headed to the foot of the mesa.

Chapter 10

The worn unofficial path began where Cade had headed, probably where hundreds of experienced hikers began making their own path. Ally knew the official path started a couple of miles up Jack's Canyon Road. Not here where the girls had followed Spike.

She moved closer taking the horses' reins and bringing them along. She'd heard of horse sense, but this was the first time she'd experienced it. They knew to stand beside her while Cade moved along the rocks, grabbing a higher one to pull himself up. She couldn't comprehend how the girls had gotten that far on their own.

As Cade made progress, the girls tried to get closer but each time they shifted back, fear tugging at their faces until she suspected tears where rolling down their cheeks. Cade's voice reached her as he spoke to the girls, telling them to stay where they were, and he would get there.

A gasp flew from her lungs when his foot slipped off a rock and he grasped onto another piece of rock to keep from slipping. For the first time in her life, adventure left her cold. Yes, this could be the kind of fun experience she would have wanted to try a couple months earlier, but now, her life had changed. Instead of adventure, she looked at danger, two sweet young girls filled with fear and their father hanging on to save them from what could be a tragic fall.

Spike, somehow, made his way down a few feet, perhaps gaining confidence from seeing a familiar face. His tail wagged the closer Cade came, and she watched the girls with trepidation that they might try to follow the dog. Her prayers rose again.

Cade stood a moment and moved sideways, apparently spotting a better path, once on it, he moved up more quickly and within another ten minutes, he'd reached the girls. They grasped him, their arms wrapping around his waist while she feared he would lose his balance and tumble down the mesa. When he crouched down to hold them close, she breathed again.

But now the task grew more difficult. Getting the girls down would not be an easy task. She wanted to be there helping them, too, but despite her love of new experiences, she cared about the girls too much to be the one who let one fall or get hurt. Today, she belonged on the ground.

Her chest tightened, and her breath thinned, as the reality of her thought struck her. She'd spent her life searching for ways to enjoy new encounters. Adventure, fun, danger clung in her mind as if she couldn't breathe without taking chances and conquering something new.

The shallowness of her goals dug into her heart, as she faced how trivial and unproductive her life had been. Again, the word legacy filled her mind. Grif expressed his realization, and when she heard him speak, the meaning of his words impacted her more than she had imagined.

Since meeting Cade and later the twins—a surprise that threw her off kilter— her goals had changed. Grif's influence had been a good one, too. One day when she leaves the earth, she longed to pass on something, something worthwhile that impacted even a few people. She didn't need to make an impression on the world, but on those who knew her well and who loved her,

Love. How rarely did that word enter her vocabulary? Sure, she loved pizza and crispy bacon, but when had she really loved a person? She worked to tolerate her parents who had made a mess of their lives and in the long run hers, but that wasn't love. She cared about Marcy, but that wasn't love either.

Love lived in the heart and soul of a person. The feeling guided a person's life in action and purpose. As she thought about it, she faced a sad truth. She'd never loved herself, not in the real sense. She looked beyond self to events and let that be who she was. Sad.

Her focus drifted upward, surprised that she'd been distracted. Surprised, at Cade's resourcefulness, she watched as he found his footing and then helped each girl move to where he stood. She grinned seeing Spike, standing beside him, too, with his tail wagging as if enjoying his adventure.

Adventure. The meaning of that word had changed for her. A dog would often tear off into the unknown chasing another dog or an animal—even a skunk. She recalled her friend's dog had done that, and it took a long time to get the stink out of the dog's fur…white fur that tended to look pink in the rain. They'd used tomato juice to neutralize the stench.

But a human without thinking could dive into their own skunk, whether it be the animal or a dangerous mistake, and live the ramifications. She been blessed to come out of her meaningless goals without damage.

"Ally." Her name arrived in unison while both girls waved at her from only a few feet up the mesa. She waved back, anxious to hear the story of how they'd ended up there, and also anxious to hug Cade for his ingenuity on getting the twins back on the ground.

When Jolie touched down, she darted toward Ally, her arms open wide and embraced her so hard she almost lost her balance. Seeing Chloe heading toward her, she stood firm and drew the child into her arms. Two seven-year-olds clung to her embrace as tears blurred her eyes. She'd never experienced such a blessing. This was an adventure worth waiting for.

Cade followed behind them, and this time, she opened her arms and ran into them. "Cade, I'm so happy for you. And proud. You handled that tenuous situation like a pro. I would have fallen apart…and actually I came close if I'm honest."

His gaze lingered on her face, and she longed to kiss his lips but with both girls clinging to them, and the dog excited and whacking them with his tail, she managed to hang on. Later, when they were alone.

Cade slipped his hand into hers. "Before we head home girls, I want to know how this happened. What caused Spike to run? I'm guessing that's what happened."

"Daddy, we didn't know he would go so far." Jolie's apologetic face tilted up to her dad's. "And when he did—"

"Spike chased a quail and her babies, Daddy." Chloe grasped his free hand to get his attention. The mama quail ran as fast as she could, but Spike stayed right behind her like cowboys do in the movies to get the cows into their pen."

"And you followed?" Cade's eyebrows arched. "Why didn't you just call him back? You shouldn't have gone after him when he went so far."

"But Daddy." Chloe's lower lip puffed forward. "He might get lost, and we were taking care of him."

Jolie slipped between them. "We did call him, but he didn't listen."

Chloe shouldered closer. "When he didn't come back—"

"We had to follow him because it was our responsibility." Jolie's face glowed. "Isn't that what you tell us?"

Cade pressed his lips together, obviously trying not to laugh. "Yes, I do like you to be responsible, but..." He blew out a stream of air as if his response would serve no purpose.

Ally bit her bottom lip, amused by the situation. "Your daddy feared you might be hurt by a wild animal. Do you know how many big animals live in this area?"

The twins glanced at each other as if they hadn't given that thought. When they looked up at her, they both nodded. "We forgot." Jolie drew closer to her with Chloe right behind.

Ally crouched down and opened her arms. "I love

you, and your daddy would be heartbroken if you'd been injured or even worse."

Chloe tilted her head. "Would your heart break, Ally?"

Words caught in Ally's throat as longing spread across the child's face. "My heart would break into a thousand pieces."

Chloe threw her arms around her as tears rolled from the child's eyes. "I love you, Ally."

"I love you, too." Jolie squeezed into the hug, and she embraced the two girls, happier than she'd been in years. Two young souls, beautiful and curious, ready to take on the world when propelled by the love they received.

She gazed up at Cade watching them with a glow she'd never seen. Before she could rise, a kiss met her cheek, and Spike gave another lap before she could escape. She and the girls burst into laughter, and Cade shook his head, a silly grin on his face.

"It's almost dinner time, and we're standing here. Let's get back and order pizza. What do you think?"

The girls jumped up and Ally dodged their clapping hands. "How will we do this, Cade?" She eyed the two horses and the four of them plus Spike. "I've never ridden with another person with me in the saddle."

"I'll show you how. The girls have ridden with me before, so they're experienced. They had an adventure that you haven't enjoyed."

A grin stole to her face. "I think I'm through with most adventures, but this one is special. Just show me what to do, and we'll get back home."

"And have pizza." Again, the two voices, like a duet, reached her ears.

She chuckled as she swung her leg over the saddle and settled her feet into the stirrups. Cade shifted to her side and lifted Jolie onto the saddle in front of her. She shifted back as far as she could to make room. "We'll go slow at a trot until we see how it's going, okay?"

Ally nodded.

Cade shifted Jolie's leg. "Jolie, watch your heels and try not to press them against the horse's shoulder."

"I know, Daddy. I let them hang down without pushing and I hang on to the saddle horn."

"Good girl." He patted her arm and stepped over to Dixie. "Ready, Chloe?"

She nodded, and he swung her onto the saddle and then slipped his foot into the stirrup and swung his leg behind her. When they were settled on the horse's back, Cade grasped Spike's leash and gave a nod. "Okay, we'll start out with a walk, and then see how we do before trotting. Okay?"

Everyone agreed, and Ally gave a signal to Bliss, and she stepped forward. When she looked across the landscape, she realized how far they had ridden earlier in the day. The ranch was blocked in part by a few other homes set more deeply in the meadow, but she knew from the sun the direction they would head.

The girls giggled, and Jolie wanted to hold the reins, so she gave in, knowing that she could control Bliss with her heel if necessary, but the child knew what she was doing and kept a tight hold but a relaxed one on the reins. "Good job, Sweetheart."

Jolie tilted her head back with a grin. "Am I really your sweetheart?"

"You and Chloe are both my sweethearts."

"What about Daddy?"

"He's my dear friend."

Jolie looked disappointed. "But not a sweetheart."

"I guess you could say he is my sweetheart too."

A smile blossomed on her face. "I love you, Ally."

"I know, and I love you too."

"And my daddy?"

The answer caught in her throat, but she had to answer. "Yes, your daddy."

"I'm glad, Ally."

Jolie quieted, and Cade tilted his head forward and picked up speed so she shifted her heel and knee, and Bliss followed along beside Dixie. Cade sent her a smile that warmed her heart. The emptiness she'd experienced for years, faded away as her chest filled with a sense of wholeness. She'd never been loved in the way she'd experienced with the girls, and with Cade. the memory of his kiss swept through her body as if the sun had slipped from behind a cloud.

Life changes tangled through her chest and around her heart. The day she ran into the nameless horseman had become the day her life had opened doors and windows that she'd never known existed.

Chloe's piping voice drew her from her thoughts, and she looked ahead to see the ranch in the far distance. The word pizza bounced into the conversation and she gathered Chloe was putting in her order. The girls brightened her life like nothing else had. Their father had illuminated her heart and soul with a glow she'd never known.

Feeling the young girl sitting astride in front of her lifted her spirit and deepened her goal. Her legacy could be the person who provided love, guidance and motivation to these two girls, who Eva announced needed a mother.

And Eva had said that Cade needed a wife. She knew Cade would survive without one, but with a wife, he had someone to share his joy and sorrows, someone to help him and be with him when he struggled, someone who kept him warm at night. The independence she'd stated as her goal shriveled into dust, and companionship and commitment became the building block of purposeful living. That would be her final adventure.

♥

Cade sent the girls inside with Spike. The neighbors would be home soon, and he was taking no chances of him running off again. Ally went inside with them and said she'd call for the pizza and salad. He'd slowed down the horses to a walk when they were still some distance from the ranch to rest the horses and save time. Riding a horse did not end when the rider returned to the ranch. He still had to care for the horses.

Each horse had gotten their full of water. The twins had given them each a bucket full and Dixie and Bliss were content. He'd unbridled the two horses and taken off the tack, and pulled out the grooming brushes, but before getting to work, he ran his hand over the horses back and legs looking for heat or sweat. He found none.

He picked up the curry brush and worked it in circular motions on both horses and finished with the stiff brush, he exchanged it for the soft one, and gave each horse a final brushing. After checking the hooves for stones or sores, he gave them both a carrot, and put the grooming supplies away.

As he finished, he heard Spike's bark and assumed the neighbors had arrived. Grateful that he'd found the girls and the dog before they'd arrived home, he headed out of the stable and strode across the yard. He shook his head when he saw the twins talking to the neighbors with so much animation, he could only imagine how panicked they were. But relief washed over him when he heard them laugh.

As he approached, Mr. Ritger gave him a smile. "I hear Spike led you on a wild ride today."

"We all enjoy a bit of old west action, and we got it."

"Thanks so much, and I'm sorry that Spike ran off. I appreciate your bringing him back."

"Thank the girls. They were the ones that followed him." Although he gave them credit, he really preferred to give him a bit of discipline, but he didn't have the heart. They were frightened enough, and he hoped had learned their lesson.

"You're a great neighbor, Cade. Thanks again." Ritger stuck out his hand and Cade shook it.

"I'd better get this mischievous dog home. He does like to chase birds and small animals. I'm not sure how to stop him, except put him on a chain, and I hate to do that."

Cade nodded, somewhat agreeing with him. "It all worked out okay so we can be thankful for that."

Ritger nodded and grasped Spike's collar. "Come on, boy. Let's go home." He gave a wave and the two struck out for the front gate.

Cade let out a sigh, in his heart, hoping Ritger didn't ask them to dog-sit again. As he headed inside, he pictured Ally with the girls. He'd told the twins to bathe and hoped they had done what he asked. They were covered with dust and red sand from the red rocks.

When he stepped inside, Ally sat in the recliner, her head back and her feet lifted on the footrest. They'd worn her out. He moved as quietly as he could across the floor, but she opened her eyes and sat straighter. "You're done?"

"I am, and I think you're done-in."

She grinned. "Worry can do that. I am so grateful the girls were okay, Cade. I don't know what we would have done if—"

"Let's not even think of that. They're here and taking baths, I hope." He settled onto a nearby easy chair.

"They are. I used the dinner delivery as a weapon."

He couldn't help but chuckle, happy that she'd already begun to learn the tactics of handling children. "Good work."

Instead of pizza, I ordered a medium antipasto salad and three spaghetti dinners with meatballs. I hope that's enough. The meals are big, and I thought the girls would share."

He nodded, though his mind had shifted a long way from dinner. "Ally, I can't thank you enough for being with me today. Having a partner by my side meant the world to me."

"I'm glad I could be there to support you, Cade. We were both paralyzed with worry, I know. You most of all."

"I saw your face. You care about my girls and I knew you were as worried as I was."

"I love those girls, Cade. It can't believe that comes so easy. You know my philosophy a few months ago. I've become a different person."

"Ally, that person was always there, but had been

covered up by a lot of baggage from the past. I know your life had been difficult, and family hadn't been that much a part of your life. But I really believe that it's part of our nature to want family and yet in certain situations, to hide from it for fear you might relive the pain you had in the past."

She nodded. "It takes time to assess the damage, Cade. But that can only happen if you recognize the damage. It's easy to deny and blame everything but the truth."

"I understand all too well. Not my parents, but Janet's death. I blamed everything on that horrible experience and figured if my life was a mess it wasn't my fault."

"What made the difference?" A deep frown wrinkled her brow.

"Reality, I suppose. My mom has opinions, and she's outspoken as you know."

Ally chuckled. "Yes, I've seen her in action and she's quite blatant about those opinions."

"Right. But you know, I'm glad she's like that in a way because each time I blamed Janet's death, my mom turned the reason around and I had to refocus on me. I would have been a rotten father without Mom's support."

"Never, Cade. I don't think you could ever be a rotten anything."

"Ally, you didn't see me back then."

"But I can see inside your heart, and you wouldn't have stayed that way. Reality would have finally come back home without your mom's help. I believe that."

"I'm glad you have such faith in me." He shrugged. "Maybe you're right, but I straightened up faster than I might have once I refocused on what was important, and it was—"

"The twins. Cade, I have no doubt."

"Right. They'd lost their mom and I couldn't let them lose their dad."

"I think that's one reason I lov…think so much of you."

Cade rose and beckoned to her. Though she gave him a questioning look, she stood and ambled his way. When she was within arms reach, he drew her into an embrace, and at her touch, he couldn't speak but lowered his lips to hers. When she responded, he deepened the kiss, and her arms slipped around his back as they melded into one body, heart beating against heart.

"Ally, I hope you know how much you mean to me and the girls. It's not my mom's version of needing a mother for the girls, but it's my version of needing someone to share my life and being beside me when things get tough and laughing with me when things are amazing."

"Cade, those exact thoughts filled my mind today. I never thought I would have a relationship with anyone that made me feel whole and complete, but I do when I'm with you and the twins. They're an extension of you, and I have feelings for them beyond anything I would have imagined."

"I see it, Ally. I couldn't believe my eyes when I realized what I had witnessed. The woman who stated adventure and fun was her life goal and look at you now."

"And look at you." She lowered her mouth to his, and his body screamed with longing that swept over him. "Ally, I—"

The doorbell jerked him back and he gave her a look that he hoped she understood. When she grinned, he knew she'd gotten the point. If it wasn't the girls, it was the doorbell.

He dug into his pocket for his wallet and then opened the door, paid the delivery man and carried in the spaghetti and salad. Before he could get the food to the table, the twins darted from their rooms and plopped down at the table. "I'm starving." Chloe grinned, and Jolie echoed her statement.

Ally joined them, and as usual, the girls took over reliving their journey with Spike and dramatized the scary parts with gusto. He tried not to laugh, but watching Ally's expression, she struggled to keep from letting out a belly laugh, too.

A lecture had to be presented to his adoring girls about wandering off without letting him know, but not tonight. They'd already let him know how frightened and sorry they were, but he felt compelled to do what a father should do and teach them right from wrong.

After they'd devoured the salad and the pasta and meatballs, he directed the girls to their room to play. "And I do not want to see your faces. I will tell you when it's bed time. Do you understand? And if you do what I'm asking, you can have milk and Ally's homemade cookies before bed."

Though their expressions had first told him they didn't like his order, their faces changed when he added the bonus. Who didn't like homemade cookies?

He knew his daughters and if he didn't stand firm, they would be hanging in the doorway with a million questions and wanting to be with Ally. He didn't blame them. He wanted to be with her too, but alone. He had so much on his mind. So much to discover.

Ally left the table with the leftovers and went to the kitchen while he watched the girls vanish. When he joined her, she had taken care of everything—dishes rinsed and stack in the sink, juice packets tossed in the trash, salad and pasta stored in the refrigerator

She motioned toward the dishwasher. "Can I put the dishes in the washer. I rinsed them."

"You did more than I do, Ally, so let me finish." He pulled open the door and set in the few dishes they'd used."

"Let's get a drink and sit in the living room."

"Water for me." She reached for a glass and poured water from the tap, then pulled out a few ice cubes from the freezer. "I'm learning my way around here."

His heart skipped. "I'm glad. That tells me you're comfortable here."

"Very, Cade. Very."

He pulled out another soda, and they settled on the sofa, their legs stretched out and their heads reclining on the seat back. "Those girls wore me out today, Ally. I'm so glad you were here for support. I forgot how wonderful it is to have someone at my side, encouraging me and calming me when I'm ready to blow a gasket."

She chuckled at his reference. "I'm glad I was here too. The girls are wonderful, but they are still kids and I guess all the training and teaching we do as parents can sometimes be waylaid by kids making their own unwise decisions. No one could blame you."

"It's not the blame that bothers me. It's the danger they were in."

"Children—even seven-year-olds—forget that danger lurks everywhere. You're right, Cade. A mountain lion, bobcat, so many other animals…and rattlers…could have attacked them, but all they saw was Spike running away and deciding it was their job to bring him back." She waddled her head back and forth. "In one way that's a good attribute, understanding responsibility, but they also forget the attribute of being careful, notifying authorities—in this case a parent— and making wise decisions. That one comes years later and sometimes—"

"Not at all." He finished her sentence.

"Right. I've made unwise decisions too often. I've not used wisdom, and I never thought about responsibility except in my job, but not in my life. My friend Marcy is a quiet yet kind and loving person. She's stuck by me during all my crazy ideas while trying to provide wisdom, but I didn't listen. I just bugged her about getting a life. But I seemed to think that her life should echo mine. We are so different, and I only looked at her with scrutiny as if I were right and she was wrong."

"We all make mistakes, Ally. But you realize what you've done, and you still have time to fix it. Ask yourself what you can do to be a real friend who respects her values and goals."

She nodded, but her expression held more meaning than the nod. "What are you thinking?"

"I have consistently tried to get Marcy to take chances and join me in my adventure seeking. She's resisted always with a reminder that we are not the same. Yet I continue to bug her. I wanted her to go on the balloon ride, to take horseback riding lessons. You name it, I bugged her."

"And she's still your friend."

Ally's eyes widened then her head lowered as if thinking. "You're right. I can't believe it. Why stick by someone who drives you crazy? Someone who doesn't seem to understand who you are?"

"I think that's what true friendship is, Ally. Friendship is a kind of love…agape love which is more than brotherly love. It's a love that shows respect, charity and even unconditional love."

Her head remained lowered. "I feel horrible, Cade. I haven't been supportive of her desire. I push her to do what I want so often. She's quiet and doesn't put herself out there to meet people and make friends, and I guess I wanted to see her enjoy life. Meet people. Date. Be loved by someone. Yet that's not something I can control or force. It just has to happen."

Cade listened while his mind shifted to his own attempts to influence others' lives. "I've done the same with Grif, Ally. He's single, and I've encouraged him to look for singles groups or join one of those groups online. I even suggested he go to a bar and look around. What kind of advice is that? It's not where I want to find a wife."

She nodded. "We seem to be desperate to help our friends find contentment and happiness, and I suppose they think they are. Although now that you mention Grif, he did say that he had no children to leave his business, no one to come home to, no one to share his legacy. Remember I told you we'd talked about legacy."

"He's never said that to me, Ally, but I'm glad you reminded me. At least, I know he's aware that his life is lonely in some ways. I like the guy, and I'd love to see him find happiness. Someone to share his experiences, even have children."

Her eyes brightened. "We could avoid interfering, but how will they meet if we don't do something?"

"Is that really our business?" Cade focused on her face.

The attention made her uneasy. "But how will they meet?"

"I don't know, but we are interfering when we get them together without telling them why?"

"No, Cade. Okay…yes. You're right. All we can do is hope somehow they meet and like each other." She flopped back against the cushion.

She sensed her disappointment, but Grif had been blunt with him and that made him think. "You know what's funny, Ally?"

"Me when I don't put on makeup."

He shook his head, controlling a chuckle, and turned to face her. "You're beautiful no matter what, but—"

"Hold it." She raised her hand to stop him. "You've never seen me without makeup."

He longed to tell her that love covered all flaws if she did have them. Instead, he returned to the question. "That's not it. This is about Grif."

"Oh." A faint frown wrinkled her brow. "I have no idea."

"Grif broke out in a laugh and asked me why he should take advice about meeting a woman when I was womanless and hadn't followed my own advice."

Her frown turned to a grin. "And what did you say?"

"Nothing. What could I say. He was right."

She brushed her hand along his cheek, her fingers rasping over his unshaven face. "You always make me smile, Cade. I've never had a relationship that has given me so much pleasure."

"You're not alone, Ally. You've changed me and my girls. I don't know what life would be if—"

"No ifs, Cade." She grasped his hand in hers and squeezed it. "I've learned so much since I met you. Not only how to laugh and enjoy life without endangering it, but I've also learned that children and companionship can be a gift and not something that stifles a person's life. I keep thinking about the girls, and all the 'what ifs' that could have happened. Now that it's over and they are safe, I realize that was excitement and an adventure that I would never want to experience again."

Her eyes glistened—tears he suspected—and he lowered his gaze to her lips, so sweet and pink, he pictured a rose bud. He lowered his mouth to hers and drank in a joy and wholeness that filled his heart. Losing Ally would tear him to bits, and soon he needed to let her know how serious he was about her. Very soon.

"Do you have any idea how much the girls care about you, Ally. They talk about you so often and want me to ask you over to play with them." He couldn't hold back a silly grin. "I've tried to explain that you're an adult and had responsibilities like a job and cleaning a house and cooking. They said they knew it, but they loved you."

"Love me." Her eyes misted again. "Cade, I've already said I adore those girls."

"I know. I can see it even if you didn't say it." He drew back and shifted his head. "Do you know what I almost forgot again? School starts in two weeks. The other day I saw an ad in the paper and it reminded me. Since they turned six, I started doing something special with them before they get back to school, and when I saw the ad for Blazin' M Wild West Ranch, I thought about taking them there."

"I've heard of it, but is it fun for kids?"

"They have all kinds of things to do, wagon ride around the ranch and into the woods, learning to lasso, silly photos, critter walk—like a petting zoo, I think. And then they have a western dinner on tin plates, and a show afterword with music and funny skits."

"Clay, that sounds cute."

"I thought so…and here's another idea. How would you like to go with us?"

"That would be fun. Sure…" Her lips pressed together, and she looked off in the distance. "Here's an idea. How about if I ask Marcy to go with me, and you invite Grif to come along and help you with the girls?"

His mind went blank. Would Grif think he was crazy? "I've never asked Grif to do anything with the girls. He might think that's weird."

"How would you know if you don't ask?"

He shrugged, having no other response. "I can try. But what about Marcy. You tell me she never wants to do things with you."

"She's good about going to the movies or shopping. I suppose they have stores there."

"They do, but you can't call it shopping. You have to pay admission. It covers the meal too."

"We've never talked about it, but I could suggest we

go. All I can do is try. If it doesn't work, then you can tell Grif that if he'd rather not go, you learned that I'm coming. That gives him an out."

"Might work. Let's give it a try."

She tilted her head and brushed a kiss over his lips. "Pick out the day and let me know. I'll invite Marcy." She paused. "We work most days so can we do a weekend or do they have this in the evening? If they service a dinner, then maybe—"

"Yes, evening. They open at five and dinner is at six-thirty. That way we won't get out too late for the twins."

"Guess what?"

He eyed her. "What?"

"I'm excited. It sounds like a fun evening just for the four of us, but it's a perfect way to include Marcy and Grif without interfering...exactly. You could tell him that I mentioned going there too, and I'll do the same with Marcy."

"Then we're sort of being honest. I like that idea." He ran his hand along the nape of her neck while his fingers brushed through her soft, shiny hair. "I could get used to this, Ally."

"So could I. We come up with some good ideas, don't we?"

He grinned. "By the way, I have another idea. Are you ready for an adventure?"

Her eyes searched his. "I'm giving up adventures, except one like the Blazin' M." She lowered her gaze as a grin formed. "At least the kind I always looked for. I've learned something else since I've met you."

Though his chest tightened, he wasn't sure why. Was it hope or concern? "I hope it's something good,

Ally."

"I think so. I've learned that experiences without a purpose aren't worthwhile. Instead, having experiences that teach something or influences my life in a good way. Now that's worthwhile."

Tension in his chest eased. "That sounds like a good philosophy."

"Going to an observatory is a way to learn about the stars and space. That could be an adventure, but it teaches something."

"Yes, those events are good. I have a chance to learn a little about air and wind currents and team work, but I hate to do it alone. What would you say to going on another hot air balloon ride?"

Her head jerk upward while her confused experience morphed to a grin. "That's right. You have two tickets." A slight frown returned. "But what about the girls?"

"Two tickets and two girls. Inviting one person makes more sense, and Grandma will gladly come for a day to spend time with them. She asked me recently when I would need her."

"Your mother is a wonderful woman, Cade." She shifted closer and touched his cheek.

He rested his hand on hers. "She's a character, too, but I love her and am grateful to have a mother who is always supportive."

"You are blessed. That's what it is."

He nodded. "So, what do you say?"

"About your mother?" She tilted her head with a toying grin.

"No, about answering my question. Will you go with me or should I give the tickets to someone else?

How about Grif and you give one to Marcy? Then we can forget the—"

"No. We have a good idea set up. Why change the plan, especially not the balloon ride? I would love to go with you."

He shifted his hand from hers and scouted closer. "I'm glad." He curved his arm around her back and drew her closer, his lips ready to meet hers, his heart ready for even more.

Ally lifted her fingers and played along his hairline while excitement tingled down his spine. Her lips opened to his, soft and sweet like ripe strawberries. She moved against his mouth, a slow circle that captured his breath as if she held his life in her hands.

When he gasped, she eased back, her lips kissing the tip of his nose, his eyes and forehead. He melted into a pool of longing, his body limp, his spirit floating on the clouds. Life without Ally dragged him to darkness. She'd become a light shining on his girls and on their father. She'd moved from neighbor to friend to the woman he wanted to spend his life with. He could only pray she felt the same.

Chapter 11

Ally eyed the clock and couldn't believe that everything had worked out perfectly. She gazed at Marcy finishing her lunch while excitement settled in Ally's mind. Today Marcy would meet Grif. "I have to go home after work, Marcy, to change clothes and do a couple things, but I'll come back and pick you up a little before five."

"If you're sure." Marcy gave her one of those I-don't-understand-you looks. "Why didn't you bring a change of clothes from home. You could change at my house?"

"I didn't think of it. You know me."

"Wow, I guess I do." Marcy gave her a playful grin. "Actually, thanks for inviting me to something fun and without danger, my friend."

"You're welcome. It's taken me a while to learn, but maybe you got through to me."

"A gift from heaven."

Ally chuckled. "I wouldn't go that far."

"I would." Marcy gathered up her lunch trash as she eyed the clock. "It's time to get back to the floor. I'll see you later then."

"Right. I think this will be fun."

Marcy nodded, picked up her tray and headed for the conveyer belt while Ally leaned back and stared into space uncomfortable with her sense of guilt. Marcy had loved the idea of going to the ranch, and now Ally faced the reality of what they had done. Though she was supposed to pick up Marcy, Cade asked Grif if he could pick up Ally's friend so she could ride with him. Marcy could blow a cork when she hears the new plans. She might even refuse to go.

With the dilemma weighing her thoughts, she pulled out her phone to call Cade. It wasn't too late to go back to the original plan. But the more she thought, Cade had made it sound workable. She'd already ordered Marcy's ticket which meant if Marcy cancelled she would have to pay for the event even if she didn't go. Marcy lived a frugal life, not extreme but thoughtful.

Ally couldn't imagine Marcy cancelling a fun time because of something that unimportant. She put the phone back in her pocket and headed back to work.

While time ticked by, Ally had taken care of all the patients being released and finished meeting with others that she'd promised to see. If she could get permission to leave a little early that would be a gift.

She spoke to the director and she agreed without a problem. Getting home early meant she could change clothes and then talk the situation over with Cade to make sure she had the information she needed. She hoped Grif had agreed to pick up Marcy since he lived in Cottonwood too.

Once home, she changed into comfortable shoes and Capris with a color-coordinated knit top. She eyed herself in the mirror, added a bit of blush and lipstick, ran a comb threw her hair, and gave a nod at herself. Not gorgeous, but then she wasn't anyway. She looked okay.

Her phone sounded before she called Cade, and she flinched fearing it was Marcy with her own problem, but Cade's number showed on her cell as she answered. "Hi. Everything okay?"

"Fine. The girls are so anxious I want to tie them up for a while, but it's getting to that time so I just wanted to make sure you call Marcy. Grif said he's happy to pick up your friend. I gave him the address you gave me so he should have no trouble finding her house. He has a GPS if he needs it."

"Okay." Her chest tightened as he spoke. "I'll call her now and say you're going too, I found out, and offered to drive me since we live so close. Then I'll tell her about Grif. I'm so afraid she'll be upset, but all I can do is let her know I have her ticket purchased already so hopefully, if she is angry, she'll ease up."

"Don't let it bother you. Grif's a great guy and he'll make her feel very comfortable. I told him she worked at the hospital and she tended to be quiet. He'll work miracles, I hope."

"So do I, Cade. I'll call her now and then I'm ready when you are. I'll tell Marcy we'll meet her by the entrance. That should work."

"Sounds good. See you in a few minutes. I'll lasso the girls and get them buckled in and we'll be on our way."

"I'm ready." She clicked off his call, and then pulled up Marcy's. Her finger trembled as she clicked the number, praying she'd sound normal."

When Marcy answered, Ally worked to steady her voice. "Hi Marcy, I'm ready to leave, but I've had a change of plans, but it should work out great."

"What do you mean?"

"Cade called right after I got home and said he and the girls are going to the Blazin' M today. Can you believe it? I did mention to him that the girls might enjoy going there some time. Anyway, when I told him we were going today, he offered to pick me up and I told him I was to go to your house. He solved the change immediately."

"So, you and Cade and the twins are coming here. Is there room in the car? I'm not comfortable."

"No, Marcy. It's not that. It's much nicer. His friend Grif planned to go with him to help keep an eye on the girls. You know how kids can get distracted and vanish. Since Grif lives in Cottonwood, it's perfect. He's picking you up instead of me. I told you he's a really nice guy. Very thoughtful. He has your address, so we'll meet you at the entrance."

"Ally, you know I'm not comfortable with that. I don't think I'll—"

"Don't say it, Marcy. I have your ticket. We'll have a great time, and you are going with us. All that's affected is the ride to the ranch, and for you it's not that far. Grif is a gentleman."

Silence hung in the air until Ally heard a deep sigh.

"I'm not happy, but you have the ticket and I'm not paying for nothing, so I'll go. But we'll talk about this later. I don't want surprises in my life. You're the one who enjoys excitement and adventure. I don't. Please remember that."

She hung up before Ally could respond, but then she didn't have anything to say anyway. She'd set up this plot to give Grif and Marcy a chance to meet, and all she could do is pray that it works out in a good way.

A single horn toot sounded as she headed for the door. She stepped outside to see the twins hanging out the side window, waving as if they hadn't seen each other for years. It made her smile. They were not only cute, but they made her heart sing.

She waved back to them, rounded the car and slipped into the passenger seat. "Everyone ready to have fun?"

"Yes." The yes was followed by two girls talking at the same time about what they wanted to do there, things Cade told them about.

"We'll all have fun. And we'll ride in a wagon pulled by a tractor all around the ranch plus into the woods. We'll have tons of fun."

"Tons." A duet repeated her word.

When the girls got distracted, she leaned closer to Cade. "I feel rotten. I tried to tell myself I wasn't lying, but it was sort of a disjointed version of the truth, and that's wrong."

"Ally, yes, but we did it for the good of two friends. We had to bend the truth a little. Still, it's a fun evening, and I anticipate that Grif and Marcy will enjoy each other's company, if nothing more."

"That's what I'm saying in my head to salve my guilt."

He laid his hand on hers. "Let's count on this being a great day."

She nodded and let the topic rest. If she let guilt overtake her, she would ruin what could be, as Cade said, a great day.

When she saw the sign for the Blazin' M Ranch, her spirit had lifted. Although she feared what she might find when they spotted Marcy with Grif, she hoped that her concern would subside. She turned her head toward the back seat. "Here we are."

The twins craned their necks looking out the window while Cade found a parking spot, and they headed for the entrance. The girls skipped along beside them. But as they approached, Ally didn't see any familiar faces. "Where are they?"

Cade scanned the area and grinned as he pointed a little to their right. She spotted Marcy and Grif deep in conversation. Her heart skipped as a breath whispered from her throat.

Cade eyed her with a wink. "I see you spotted our friends."

She grinned back. "But I don't think they see us. They're preoccupied."

He slipped his arm around her and beckoned the girls to follow them. As they drew nearer, Grif raised his arm in a wave. Marcy turned toward them, a contradiction of guilt and innocence on her face. She shifted away from Grif and gave a shy wave. "Hi. Did you just arrive?"

"Yes, and we didn't see you at first." Ally moved to her side and lowered her voice. "Thanks for not being upset."

"I understood. Your plan made more sense than my discomfort." She eased away from Grif's ear while Cade and the girls took over his attention. "He is a very nice man. Very kind and thoughtful. He opened the car door for me, can you believe it?"

"I can with Grif. He's one in a million when it comes to chivalry."

Marcy gave a little nod, and then motioned toward the group. "I suppose we should go in. I think they're waiting."

Relief spread through Ally's chest, and she beckoned the others to move to the entrance gate. They all headed inside with their tickets and stood to gaze at all the shops and events that they could enjoy.

Chloe was the first to spot her interest. "Can we go over to see the pets?"

Jolie poked her sister. "Critters, that's what they're called here." She looked up to her dad for confirmation.

Cade shook his head. "Pets or critters. But yes, the advertisement calls them critters."

"See, Chloe, I was right." Jolie's cute little nose turned up a bit and Ally had to muzzle a chuckle.

Cade halted the conversation. "I have an idea. Why don't we get in line for the wagon tour of the ranch? Then we'll see everything that's here, and we can decide what we're going to do. How's that sound?" He pointed to the tractor with the wagon attached filling up with passengers.

"That sounds fun to me." Ally jumped in to support Cade's idea.

Grif eyed Marcy. "How's that sound to you?"

"I think it would be fun. I've never been on a wagon ride before."

Grif chuckled. "I think we have to turn you into a cowgirl, Marcy. All cowgirls have been on a hay wagon at least once in their life."

She grinned. "Then maybe it's time for me to learn something new."

Ally yanked her moon eyes back to normal. Marcy startled her when she jumped at the idea of learning something new. She faced one thing as she'd thought about this meeting. Don't make a big deal out of anything Marcy says or does. Drawing attention to it could ruin Marcy's fun and chance to spread her wings.

Cade led the way to the line and conversation continued until a tractor pulled up with an empty wagon. The twins couldn't stand still as they moved forward, and when they climbed on the girls sat together near the front while Marcy and Grif sat a few rows back on the other side. She and Cade found seats one row back on the other side so they could keep an eye on them.

The tractor moved, and the wagon gave a jerk and rolled along behind it as the driver pointed out the sights and events that made the ranch fun for all. They passed old west farm equipment and critters, and a grave yard memorializing old west characters.

When the ride ended, the girls wanted to learn to rope, and Cade and she knew it was nearly impossible, they guided the girls to the activity. Marcy had her eye on some of the gift shops, and Grif joined her. Ally's heart fluttered, anticipating what might happen now that the two had met.

During the rounds, Grif convinced Marty to go into the jail so he could take a photo of her, and they laughed when Cade insisted both of them go to jail and he captured the photo. Time flew, and after they had experienced many of the opportunities, the dinner bell rang, and people hurried to get in line.

Inside they were given a metal plate and followed the line through the kitchen where chicken and ribs were doled onto their plates, baked potato wrapped in foil, cowboy beans, coleslaw made from prickly pears, biscuits and for dessert, Apple Carmel crisp served on ice cream. They entered the dining area and found six seats together, close enough to the stage to have a good seat for the entertainment.

"Yummy!" The girls giggled as they gnawed on the ribs, ate the beans and potatoes, and rejected the coleslaw. Both turned up their noses. Chloe pointed to the treat. "I need room for dessert."

"Me, too." Jolie nibbled on a biscuit with a piece of chicken sticking out the sides.

"I can't believe how much you girls can eat." Ally widened her eyes while she teased them.

"We have to eat, Daddy says, so we can grow." Jolie eyed her daddy.

"But you don't have to eat the tin plate."

Chloe giggled and so did everyone else.

Seeing Marcy and Grif laughing and chatting touched Ally's heart. She longed for Marcy to enjoy life, but then she reminded herself that what she enjoyed wasn't necessarily what someone else would want or need. Yet this time, she's been correct. The look in Marcy and Grif's eyes assured her they were having a good time.

As the meal ended, the show began with music, jokes and skits. She'd worried the girls would get tired and start to whine, but her fear had been wasted. The two girls clapped their hands, laughed at the silly skits, and they sang Ghost Riders in the Sky to end the program. They were glued to the window where they heard that a Ghost Rider would gallop passed the windows. They weren't disappointed, when the eerie figure, gauzy white robe fluttered on the wind.

The clamor of applause and good comments filled the air as they left the building and headed to their cars. No one seemed disappointed. In fact, they had all agreed it was the most fun they'd had in a long time.

Marcy said good night without a qualm as she followed Grif toward the parking lot. Ally watched as he eventually took her arm as she looked up at him talking as if they'd been friends a lifetime.

"Cade, I'm so happy." She tilted her head toward the couple.

"We did good, Ally."

"Me?" Jolie butted in apparently thinking the reference was about the twins.

"You were good too, Jolie. You and Chloe, but we were talking about us."

Their brows wrinkled as they gazed at them, obviously not understanding. "Did you do good too, Daddy?"

"We did, Chloe. Everyone here did good, don't you think?"

Two heads pumped their agreement, and by then they'd reached the car. Moments after they pulled onto the highway, Jolie and Chloe had fallen asleep. The quiet wrapped around Ally's heart, aware of the love she felt for the girls, something she never believed possible. "Do you hear that?"

Cade glanced her way. "Hear what?"

"Nothing. Only silence."

He flashed a grin while keeping his focus on the road. "It's been a great day, Ally. I love seeing you and the twins together. You've become a real role model for those girls."

"I'm not trying to step into their mother's shoes, Cade. She will always be their mom. I'm only helping them to remember what mother's do."

"You might not be their birth mother, Ally, but they were young when Janet died, and they see you as someone important in their lives. I'm not trying to scare you or make you feel compelled to be something you don't want to be. I just mean—"

"Cade, I know what you mean, and you can stop worrying. Your daughters have changed my life in a good way. My self-centered world has drifted past me, and I'm grateful. Now the fun and excitement and adventure I used to seek involves not just me, but the people I love. Your two beautiful daughters included."

She noticed him press his lips together as his eyes misted, even evident from his profile. "Cade, you are part of that too. You know that."

"Both of our lives have changed, Ally. And in an amazing way."

They settled into silence, and as he turned onto Beaver Head Flat Road, her mind soared with the hopes and dreams that filled her. Dreams she never wanted and hopes she never believed. She shifted a little closer, though hindered by the seatbelt, wanting to be part of him, longing to face the world together. She'd been alone a long time, and she'd lost the desire to stay that way. Though she could only hope that Cade felt the same, questions niggled her, ones she hoped would be answered soon.

♥

Cade dropped the girls off at school and returned to

the quiet house. Summer had been special with Ally being part of it. Her wonderful interest and treatment of the girls touched him, and roused his hope that Ally cared about him as much as he cared for her.

Overwhelmed by the silence, he headed to the stable to muck the stalls, and he needed to move three or four horses into the corral for exercise. As he walked them to the enclosure, he spotted a vehicle pulling up the road. He waved when he recognized Grif's four-wheeler.

When he moved the horses into the corral, he locked the gate as Grif left his jeep and strolled over to him. "How's it going?"

"Good. Just letting the horses get out a bit. What's up with you?"

Grif grinned. "I'm taking Marcy to dinner tomorrow night."

"Great. I'm glad you two enjoyed each other's company. Ally said she was a nice woman. Just a bit quiet."

"Not when you get to know her. We've had some good laughs, and you know...I'd been thinking that..." He waved the words away. "It's just nice to have someone to spend time with. Life can drag on if you let it."

"It can, and even when it's busy, Grif. Busy doesn't make up for companionship. I'm glad you two got along so well."

Grif adjusted his hat. "I suspect that Ally hoped that we'd get along. Marcy told me that Ally's always bugging her to get out and enjoy life."

Cade couldn't deny it, but he didn't agree. "Ally often worries about other people, since she loved to seek out adventures."

"I remember her saying that, but seeing Ally now…hmm? I think something has changed."

He nodded. "I see it, too. The other day she said that her self-centered world has drifted away. It has. I've watched it happen. Now she said the adventure she always wanted was no longer self-focused and involved more than her. Now it involved the people she loves. She mentioned the girls." He pressed his hand against his heart. "That got to me, Grif."

"I can understand why." He drew in a lengthy breath. "A while ago, I talked to Ally about legacies. That idea seemed to surprise her. I don't think she ever thought about what she'd leave to the world after she was gone. I know I have material things, but no one to leave them to either, so I understood her surprise. I think that discussion changed both of us. I do want to have a life that's more than running a ranch and owning a store. I want family and someone to share it with."

Cade nodded, his mind flying with his own wants. "I have the girls to leave the ranch to, but that doesn't totally fulfill my life either. The last part of what you said is where I'm at, Grif. I want someone to share it with."

"Ally?" Grif's eyes searched his.

"I think it's obvious how I feel about her, and I think she cares about us, but love? Now that's another thing. I need to act and do it soon, Grif. At times, I'm confident that she has strong feelings for me, but is that something that brings about a commitment, a partnership, a…a future together. Someone to cuddle with at night and to stand beside you in life's storms. I haven't asked her yet, but I'm ready. Asking her is in the air."

"In the air?" Grif gave him a quizzical look. "Like you're floating on the clouds."

Cade couldn't help but chuckle. "Sort of. Just wait. You'll see."

"Now I'm curious. Is this all I'm going to get." Grif put his fist against his hip. "Come on. We've been friends a long time."

"We have. You're right." Cade held his ground. "Another sunset and sunrise. Soon."

"You're driving me crazy, Cade."

"That's a short drive, Grif."

Grif gave him a playful punch and seemed to give up.

"Where are you going to dinner?"

"You mean where am I taking Marcy?"

Cade nodded.

"I'm not sure. I think I'll give her choices. Ask her if she has a favorite restaurant. Maybe Stromboli's if she likes Italian or Plaza Bonita for Mexican."

"Wise to give the lady a choice."

Grif shrugged. "You know me, Cade. I'm not that confident with women, but Marcy is quiet and yet we talk a lot and she's a nice woman. She made it clear she'd not looking for anything, but she's willing to have someone for company. That's all I want for now, too."

"Then it worked out well for you. I'm glad Marcy came along."

"Me, too." Grif tried to hide a grin but he failed. "So, I'm not getting anything more from you on that 'air' line, right?"

"Right. My head is in the clouds right now, Grif."

"I guess I'll either have to join you in the clouds or

be patient."

Cade grasped his shoulder. "Patience works. Just hang on and look up."

Grif tilted his head toward the sky. "Hmm? I do see a few clouds."

"You missed something." Cade pointed off in the distance. "You missed that."

Grif followed the direction of his finger. "Ah, a hot air balloon. Only a nut would take a chance with his life in a wicker basket carrying a lighted propane tank and held up by a plastic balloon."

"I often thought the same thing, Pal. But they are pretty in the sky."

"I suppose." He shifted backward and shook his head. "I better let you get back to work. I came to Sedona on business, and I need to be on my way too."

Cade flopped his arm around Grif's shoulder. "Glad you stopped by. I'll see you soon, I'm sure."

Grif lifted his hand in a goodbye and headed for his car.

Cade watched Grif climb in and head out the gate, but his mind still hung in the air and that reminded him that he needed to call Ally.

He shifted to the porch, pulled out his phone and sat on a step before he punched in the call. The phone rang a few rings, and he feared she wasn't able to answer, when he heard the line open. "Hi Cade. Is everything okay?"

"Sure is. The girls started school today so it's too quiet here."

She chuckled. "It won't be when they get home."

"I'll keep that in mind." He couldn't help but chuckle. She knew his girls. "The reason I called is about the balloon ride. I almost forgot to tell you that I made the reservation a couple days ago. It's tomorrow morning. Did I get it right?"

"You did. That's the day I arranged to be absent. Are you getting excited?"

"I'm not sure you can call it that."

"Oh, I thought maybe—"

"Nervous is more accurate."

She gave a loud giggle. "You're kidding me. You're a tough horseman, and you're nervous about a balloon."

"The balloon is fine, Ally. The problem is me in a basket a mile above the earth."

Another snicker. "It's safe. I promise. Trust me."

Her "trust me" caught his attention. "Okay, I will trust you. We'll see how it goes."

Even if you're not excited, I am. It'll be fun watching you on your first ride in a wicker basket floating with the clouds. And I promise we're not headed for the Emerald City."

"Now, I'm disappointed." This time he chuckled at their silliness. "By the way, Grif stopped by. He said he enjoyed Marcy's company, and especially that neither of them are looking for anything more than someone to do things with."

"Really, I thought maybe…"

"Are you disappointed? We can never plan someone's future. We just gave them the opportunity to meet each other."

"You're right, Cade, and that was successful. And who knows."

"Very true. Anyway, you're at work, so I'll let you go. See you later. We need to talk about the details for the ride—when we're leaving and if we need to take anything. Remember I'm new at this."

"How about tonight. We can talk then. Until later, Cade."

He said goodbye and clicked off the call, wishing he'd said so much more. He hoped she knew how deeply he cared about her. Tonight he had to talk with the girls. They needed to know how he felt too, and what he planned to do about it.

Chapter 12

Though the autumn weather in Sedona was always pleasant, the morning air sent a chill down Cade's back. He'd stopped for Ally and drove to the location to be picked up by the balloon crew. Though he had second thoughts about the balloon ride, he didn't have second thoughts about his time with Ally. Anxiety and excitement wrestled for his attention.

"I think you'll be amazed, Cade." Ally rested her arm against his as if she still wished she were at home in bed.

"I know it must be interesting, but I made a mistake with not bringing a sweater. I'm guessing it's colder up there than it is down here."

"You won't notice anything but the view and the experience. I promise."

He slipped his arm around her back and gave her a hug. "You said what I wanted to hear."

She nestled closer. "What are you doing about the

girls in case we're not back early enough?"

"You know my mom. When I told her about the ride, she sounded a bit concerned but then said, she knew you wouldn't steer me wrong. You've gotten another notch from my mom."

"I do like Eva. She has good taste." She chuckled. "But seriously, she is more supportive than so many parents are, Cade. You've been blessed."

"I have and even more than that, Mom's coming to the house and will pick up the girls from the school bus stop and stay until we're back. I couldn't ask more than that."

"You couldn't. She's a treasure."

A chill ran down his back, but he hoped he hid it from Ally. He didn't want to be a wimp and his big question had to do with being actually cold or being petrified. He settled for cold.

A moment later, the van pulled in front of them, and the door opened with a wave from one of the workers to climb in. He gave Ally a boost and joined her in the second seat. The back seat held another couple. Ally stuck out her hand "I'm Ally, and this is Cade. Is this your first trip in a balloon?"

"It is." The man stuck out his hand. "Jean and I'm Ben. How about you?"

Cade shook his head. "I hate to admit but this is my first trip, but not Ally's, and what she tells me, this will be an amazing experience."

Jean finally spoke. "That's what we heard."

As they rode, they all grew silent. Cade slipped Ally's fingers between his and rubbed her soft flesh with his thumb. He loved touching her small hand swallowed by his rougher hands that he feared might rasp against her tender skin.

"You're quiet, Ally. Is something wrong?"

She turned with a sweet grin. "No, I'm thinking how nice it will be to share one of my adventures with you."

He lowered his voice. "I'm guessing with only two others, we can still turn and look in every direction."

Though she nodded in agreement, looking only at her filled his mind. Ally didn't realize how beautiful she was in his eyes. The shape of her face, her golden wheat-colored hair, her eyes that changed from green to tan in the light. Her lips, soft and full, ready to be kissed. Everything about her, and even more, she was beautiful inside too. And his daughters loved her as much as he did.

"Here we are." The driver slowed and pulled onto an open field. The basket stood near them, and on the other side, he saw a mammoth balloon stretched out on the ground, fluttering with the air being pumped inside.

Their door opened, and he exited first and helped Ally to the ground. He couldn't help but stare at the wicker basket, one he would ride into the sky a mile high and sail to who knew where. As he'd learned, the balloon followed the wind so the pilot's only control was heading up or down with no control over the direction. The journey depended on the wind.

Ally slipped her hand into his and squeezed. "What do you think?"

"Do you really want to know?"

She nodded and grinned.

"I think I'm nuts, but then you've vouched for this experience so I'm trusting you."

She cuddled to his side and rested her head on his

shoulder. "That's all I needed to hear."

Within minutes the large propane blower went to work, the balloon began to buoy upward, slowly but as it raised, the basket attached tipped upward. "Gather round." He beckoned them to get closer. "In a moment, you'll use these slits in the wicker to climb into the basket, but before we do, I'll read the Balloonist's Prayer."

Ally placed her hand on the basket, so he followed. The pilot joined them and touched the wicker basket as he read:

> *May the winds welcome you with softness.*
> *May the sun bless you with its warm hands.*
> *May you fly so high and so well*
> *that God has joined you in laughter*
> *and set you gently back again*
> *into the loving arms of Mother Earth.*

"Now, climb in and get ready for an amazing ride."

The pilot hopped in before Cade could move. As he helped Ally into the basket, the pilot lit the propane tanks under the balloon and as fire shot upward, Cade felt a pull on the basket. Without hesitation, the balloon began to lift. As he watched the van and crew begin to shrink, his heart skipped. Today his life would change, God willing.

Ally's face glowed, and her eyes focused on him rather than the sight below.

"Don't spend the time watching me. Let's watch the landscape together."

"But I love your face. You look really happy, Cade."

"I am. I'm sitting on top of the world." He gave her

a wink.

Ally wobbled her head with a grin. "You're not sitting, my dear. You're standing."

"Just as good." He glided his arm around her shoulders and drew her closer to him, as he looked out across the expanse of red rocks, mountains and open meadows with an occasional house setting along a road. "Amazing."

"It is. Do you feel us move?"

"No. Not at all. It's as if we are standing still and the rest of the panorama is on a conveyer belt."

She tilted her head toward his face. "I told you. It's amazing, isn't it?"

"Not as amazing as you are, my love. Not by a long shot." He lowered his lips to hers with a swift kiss.

He looked toward the ground trying to calculate how high up they'd flown. "Is this a mile yet?"

The pilot glanced at him. "Not yet. It'll be a while." The guy gave him a questioning look.

"I was just curious." And anxious. But he kept that to himself.

He shifted closer to the basket edge, gazing down at the curves and rugged slabs of rock jutting from the amazing red rock formations. Familiar shapes caught his attention but from a different view. Looking down, he saw the crags, rugged caverns and scattered vegetation that he'd paid little attention to before.

He turned to Ally. "I see now why you were impressed with the ride. Things look different from up here." His statement faltered with another thought. "But not everything. You're as gorgeous as you always are and as wonderful."

Her eyes searched his. "I feel the same, Cade, and

this ride is more precious to me, because you are here, and the girls are waiting for us down below."

He drew her into his arms, longing to stay that way forever.

"We're a mile high." The pilot's voice jolted his thought.

"Thanks. That's what I was waiting for." His heart skipped and then thumped through his chest, and his hand shook as he dug into his pocket.

Ally shifted back. "Waiting for what?"

He didn't answer.

"Cade. You're not making sense." Her brow wrinkled as she studied him.

"I make sense, Ally. I know what I mean." His lighthearted response didn't change her expression. "I'm teasing."

"Okay, but I still don't—"

"You will." As the words left him, she tilted his head and he gazed into her startled face. "Ally, I can only pray that you feel about me as I do about you. My life, before I met you, was good. I had my daughters and the ranch. I love my girls, and they love me, but it's not the kind of love I longed for."

Her gaze shifted from his eyes to the world far below, and then sought his gaze again.

"When I met you, Ally, I realized what it was I yearned for. It was someone like you who would share my joys and sorrows, my good days and bad. Someone who would sit beside me and talk about our day and curl up with me at night. I missed having a precious woman tell me she loved me, and that's why…" He lowered his knee to the basket floor and moved his hand forward that was holding the box.

"Ally, I'm asking you to be my wife. To marry me and my daughters."

He heard a gasp from Jean as she caught Ben's arm and they shifted as far back as they could.

Ally stood silent, her eyes shifting from the pilot to Jean and Ben, and then to him before her startled expression melted to a warm glowing smile. "Cade. I fell in love with you a long time before I realized how I felt. I missed you when we were apart. I thought of you when I was at work, and home pretending to be content, and yet all I wanted to do was be with you, and with Chloe and Jolie. But that's what bothers me."

His neck shot backward, and he rose. "The girls bother you? But I thought—"

"Not bother me in a bad way. Your life is their life, and I don't want to step into your home and take over their world without their—"

"Ally, do you think I would ask you without having talked to the girls first?"

Her eyes widened. "You did?"

"I did."

She stood a moment as if uncertain. "What did they say?"

"They clapped and laughed and screamed and cried with happiness. I wish you had been there."

"Really, Cade. Are you sure that—"

"Trust me, Ally. Trust me."

She stepped into his arms. "I do. I do trust you with my heart, my love, my life. And I adore your girls. The adventurous woman looking for excitement found it right on your doorstep, Cade, and I never want to leave."

He lowered his lips to hers, his heart higher than the

mile they'd soared. When he eased back, he raised the box and lifted the lid. "Ally, will you marry me and accept this ring as a symbol of our love."

As if the blue velvet box had surprised her, she gazed at it unmoving as tears glistened on her lashes.

He lifted the ring from the box, and her eyes widened as she gazed at the sparkling diamond in a gold setting.

"Cade, it's beautiful. It glistens like sunshine on the morning dew."

He extended the ring toward her, and she offered her hand. After he slipped the ring on her finger, he drew her into his arms. "I love you more than I can say in words, Ally."

"Cade, I love your girls and I love you. Not only love you but respect you and admired all you've done raising those darling girls and running a business. You are an amazing man and father, and I am so thrilled and ready to be your wife and a caregiver to your girls."

"A caregiver? Ally, be prepared. You'll be far more than that to those girls."

"However they see me, Cade, is fine with me. And yes, I'll be your wife forever."

At those words, applause sounded behind them with congratulations from Ben and Jean and even from the pilot.

Her lips met his and their arms entwined, as her mouth moved on his as sweet and soft as chocolate truffle. His body warmed with the thought of Ally as his wife.

When she eased back, he studied her face, picturing her across from him in the morning at breakfast and lying beside him at night. "Are you ready to name a date, Ally?"

Her expression blossomed to a grin. "How about tomorrow?"

"That long? I'm not sure I can wait."

Ben and Jean let out a titter, and the pilot made a guttural sound before he laughed. "Congratulations, both of you, but let's wait until we get back on the ground. I don't have a license to officiate a marriage."

Cade chuckled. "Good idea. I suppose we have family who might like to attend." He brushed Ally's cheek.

She laid her hand on his. "Especially two daughters who would never forgive us if they were left out."

"You're right." He drew her close again as they stood in silence looking at the world below them and the sky above. He'd joked about being on top of the clouds, and today he'd come closer to heaven than ever before and with the woman he loved.

♥

Ally couldn't focus on their landing and the champagne toast and the final Balloonist prayer. Over and over, she heard Cade's deep, loving voice propose to her, something she'd never anticipated until the past months when she met Cade and his girls. Her life did a huge twist, and her happiness grew each day being with them.

Cade seemed to enjoy the flight and had some laughs getting out of the basket when they landed, but she'd been too preoccupied to ask what he thought.

The crew dropped them off near Cade's gate, and that's where she longed to be. Cade's mom and the girls would be waiting for them to return, and her heart pounded anticipating what they would say. Cade's confidence that everyone was thrilled had pleased her, but seeing it with her eyes hung in her mind since he'd proposed.

Her anxiety startled her, and yet helped her face the empty life she'd led before Cade appeared on horseback months earlier. She'd tacked his cowboy persona as another opportunity for adventure rather than realizing she had just faced the man who would change her life for the better.

"You're quiet." Cade squeezed her hand. "Are you okay? I hope you're not having second thoughts about—"

"I hope you don't mean that, Cade. I'm the happiest woman in the world at this moment. I'm quiet because I'm facing how empty and useless my life was until I met you. I have a world full of catching up to face and I'm so very happy. I adore you. I love your mom and the girls. I couldn't be more thrilled and ecstatic."

He glanced down the driveway, paused and drew her to him. "Then let's put the final touches on my proposal and your yes."

His lips met hers, tender and sweet, and then deepened with urgency and amazing love she had never felt in her life. She surrendered to his kiss, moving and lingering until she could no longer breathe. When he eased back, their eyes met, the longing evident. The wedding would be soon, she had no doubt. They had both waited years to let themselves be guided to their soul mate and she had no doubt, their relationship would be blessed.

Cade lifted his fingers and brushed her cheek. "Before my mother tries to run down the driveway with the girls, we'd better get up to the house."

She laughed at the picture he'd painted. They joined hands, and before they were halfway, Chloe and Jolie shot from the house, their screams almost echoing against the red rocks and flew toward them. They both opened their arms as Jolie dived into her's and Chloe into Cade's. With a huge hug and a kiss on the cheek, she shifted back and eyed both girls.

"Why are you so excited?" She tried to hide her grin.

"Because you're going to be…" Both pairs of eyes glanced at their father with question.

"She said yes, girls."

"Yes!" Duet voices yelled into the sky.

Ally bit her lip to not laugh. If a tree filled with birds had been nearby, the sky would have been filled with their panic. When she looked up, she saw Eva making her way down the driveway.

"We'd better head to the house girls. Cade, your mom is heading down here."

"Okay, ladies let's head for Grandma."

The two turned like a flash of lightning darting toward Eva, their voices bellowing what they'd learned. "She said yes, Grandma. She said yes."

Cade slipped his arm around her waist and they followed the girls up the driveway, both chuckling as they hurried.

"Ally." Eva opened her arms and bound toward her. "I'm so happy. You've answered my prayers, and the girls' prayers too."

"And Cade has answered mine, Eva. I couldn't ask for anything better in the whole world. Your son and your two beautiful granddaughters."

Tears glistened in Eva's eyes and Ally found her

own blurring her vision. She took Eva's hand and they followed Cade and the twins up the driveway to the house.

Inside, Cade offered drinks and tried to shush the girls so they could get a word in, but they finally gave up until Cade brought out some snacks with the offer to take them all out for dinner.

Eva asked about the balloon ride, and Ally enjoyed hearing Cade's description of the ride since after the proposal, they hadn't even mentioned the experience.

"It was like standing still in the air, Mom, while the world slid past us. You can't believe it until you go on one."

Eva tittered. "I think I'll pass."

Cade continued and when he mentioned reaching a mile high, he described the proposal and all that happened. The girls finally sat still and listened. Ally wasn't sure if it happened, because they wanted to hear about the proposal or they were too busy eating potato chips.

"And you said yes, Ally." Chloe stood and headed for her and Jolie jumped up not wanting to be left behind.

"I did say yes."

Jolie grasped her hand. "You will be Daddy's wife."

Chloe made a snort sound. "When people get married, Jolie, that's what happens. Are you that—"

"Girls." Ally shifted her head to look at both of them. "We're all excited, so let's be kind to each other okay."

Chloe lowered her head with a nod, and Ally put her arm around both girls. "Yes, I will be your daddy's wife, and I will live with you in this house."

"And will you be our mother?" Chloe almost whispered the question.

"I will be whatever you want me to be, Chloe. I can be your caregiver, your adult friend, or—"

"Our mother. We want you to be our mother." This time Jolie spoke.

"I've never been a mother, so you'll have to help me."

Both girls tilted their heads. "How?"

"We'll see. I'll have to learn what you'd like me to do to be a good mother."

"Love us." Jolie's look broke her heart.

"I already do that, Jolie. I love both of you and have for a long time."

Chloe elbowed into the conversation. "I told you Jolie."

"Girls." Cade gave them a look but they missed it, although they didn't miss his tone of voice.

"We can talk about this later, girls, but first we have something very important to do."

"Eat dinner." Chloe's response caused everyone to laugh, even Chloe.

"That too, but I was referring to the wedding. We have to get married first."

"Can we do it tomorrow?" Jolie's eager voice stirred another laugh.

"Soon, but not tomorrow." She opened her arms wide and each girl snuggled into one side. "You can be part of the wedding too."

"We can?" A duet question sailed past her.

"You can but let's talk about dinner and let your daddy say what he has to say and your grandma. No one has had a chance."

The twins tittered and remained tucked into her arms.

Her heart warmed to a spring day, and her joy reached higher than the mile…almost to heaven. She had never considered herself worthy of marriage. She didn't think she could handle it, not after her upbringing, but somehow, life had a way of teaching lessons and God had a way of guiding people to reach for the stars. She'd found her stars. In fact, she'd found the universe and she could only say thank you over and over for the love and happiness that she'd been given as a gift. Who knows what life holds in store until we take steps and take chances.

Ally had finally found the adventure and excitement she'd sought all her life, and it was right in front of her, almost on her doorstep.

The beginning

Dear Reader

Since moving to the Southwest, Sedona, Arizona, I have been stimulated by a different lifestyle. Instead of an urban area in the Midwest with tall buildings and elm and maple trees, here I am in a small town in the desert, surrounded by red rocks and cacti. I love it here, and the landscape and lifestyle has affected the stories I write. I've never written a book set on a ranch with horses and surrounded by mountains. I hope you enjoyed the new setting and with Cade and Ally who didn't expect to fall in love. I enjoyed introducing you to Jolie and Chloe, the twin 7-year-olds. In my next book, you will revisit these characters as you learn more about Marcy and Grif, two people with no plan to fall in love. I also love to share recipes with you, so below you will find the great easy to make cookie that Ally made. It's also glutton free. I hope you give it a try and enjoy it.

Flourless Peanut Butter Cookies
Makes 4 - 5 dozen cookies
Oven 350 degrees

Ingredients*

1 cup peanut butter
3/4 cup packed brown sugar
1 large egg
3/4 tsp. baking soda
*If dieting, you can use low fat peanut butter and Splenda brown sugar

Directions
Beat all ingredients until well mixed. Drop by tsp, 1-1/2

inches apart on parchment paper lined cookie sheets. Bake until puffed and starting to get light brown on the edges, about 8-10 minutes.

Cool 5 minutes then transfer to wire rack. Enjoy

About Gail

Best-selling and award-winning novelist, Gail Gaymer Martin is the author of contemporary romance and romantic suspense with 81 published novels and over four million books sold. Her novels have won numerous national awards, including: the ACFW Carol Award, RT Reviewer's Choice Award and Booksellers Best. Gail is the author of Writer Digest's *Writing the Christian Romance.* She is a founder of American Christian Fiction Writers and a member of Advanced Speakers and Writers. Gail is a keynote speaker at churches, civic and business organizations and a workshop presenter at conferences across the U.S. She lives with husband Bob in Sedona, AZ. Contact her by mail at: PO Box 20054, Sedona, AZ 86341 or on her website or social media.

Website:www.gailgaymermartin.com
Facebook:www.facebook.com/gail.g.martin.3
Twitter:http://twitter.com/GailGMartin
GoodReads: http://bit.ly/1e8Gt6D
LinkedIn: www.linkedin.com/in/gailgaymermartin

Gail's Books from Winged Publication

Novels - *Reissues*
Dreaming of Castles 2014
Out On A Limb 2016
Over Her Head 2017
Love Comes To Butterfly Tree Inn 2017
A Love Unforeseen 2017
Loving Treasures
Loving Hearts

Loving Ways
Loving Care
Loving Promises
Loving Kisses
Loving Arms
Teacher's Pet (Former: Dad in Training)

Novels - New
Treasures Of Her Heart 2014
Romance By Design 2015
Mackinac Island Christmas 2017
Love in the Air

Novellas   Reissues
An Open Door
Apples Of His Eye
Better To See You
Once A Stranger
Then Came Darkness
To Keep Me Warm
True Riches
Yuletide Treasures

Novellas - New
Lattes and Love Songs 2015
Apple Blossom Daze 2016
A Trip To Remember 2016
A Tucumcari Christmas 2016
Poppy Fields and You, 2017
Love Comes to Butterfly Tree Inn 2017
Tumbling Into Love 2017
Lost In Red Rock Country 2017
Autumn's Fresh Beginnings 2017

Collections
Christmas Potpourri

Forget Me Not Romances #1
Forget Me Not Romances #2
Love Blooms In The Here & Now
Mocha Marriage
Romance Across the Globe
Romance On The Run
Seven Mysterious Ladies
With This Ring
A Kiss is Still a Kiss
Get Your Kiss On Route 66
Valentine Matchmakers
All Mixed Up
Love In Danger
California
Second Change At Love
When Love Calls
The Hope of Christmas
Happily Ever After
Romancing The Wild
Returning Home
Coming Home Again
Songs of the Heart
Fall N' For You
Stranded